SICKLE

THE FERAL COURT, BOOK IV

MYRA DANVERS

FOREWORD

Make sure you sign up for Myra's Newsletter so you never miss sexy NSFW art, free things, exclusive deals, and loads of other cool shit you do not want to miss.,.

Sign up for Myra's Newsletter today!

This book is dedicated to boobies.

Who sets a goddamned preorder, gets pregnant, horribly sick for 9 months straight, has a ridiculously cute kid, and also writes a book?

This guy.

I've been weeping into my calendar for 13months straight.

Everything I own is wet with my own author tears, and it's sum bullllshit, lemme just say.

1

Warbling low in her throat, her red frill in full flare about her tiny, furious face, a female lava-kin stood her ground. Guarded on all sides by male siblings, she was a perfect replica of the corpse outside. A ferocious predator, born to kill.

She lunged, issuing a single, cooing bark that sent the males into five identical coils.

Sickle lurched back, staggering away from the tiny wryms who watched his every hasty movement. Pupils thin slashes of alien spite, theirs was a glare of primal hatred mixed with a dash of hesitation. The fear of juveniles who lacked the confidence to strike.

A burst of embarrassed laughter bubbled up, and, tracked by half a dozen ravenous glares, Sickle allowed himself a moment to breathe. To laugh in the face of all that ravenous loathing—at himself, for though the lava-kin clutchlings would one day be the most fearsome predators in all the great beyond, that day had not come.

Peering down his nose, he towered above the tiny, starving creatures and knew a brief instant of empathy for the things that would make his next meals.

"Sorry," he whispered and kicked out a booted foot when the frilled female puffed up her neck and one of the males feinted toward his left. "Not today. Not by you."

Setting his attention to more pressing concerns, the Omega male turned—his nape aching with the reminder of Balkazar's claws set deep into his flesh. Balkazar, who'd been infected and had meant to kill Sickle for daring to reach for freedom. For daring to defend himself from rape and a gruesome death.

But defend himself, he *had*.

Sickle grinned through the hurt, despite the lingering worry and the fear that he too had been infected as the others had. Pleased by the plump, rounded sense of justice, that he'd gotten vengeance on the war chief who might have killed them both. Balkazar could try as hard as he wished, run as fast as his long, Anhur legs might carry him, and still, he couldn't escape the gaping maw of fate.

He'd be swallowed by the horde. Either to live within it or to die beneath it. Just another causality no one would ever think to record.

None but Sickle, who'd been the engineer of Balkazar's end.

Baring the points of his teeth, Sickle's grin grew feral as he recalled the moment Balkazar had finally realized himself outmatched. Beaten by a lowly Omega male who wasn't strong or fast. Who hadn't been born with the coveted Anhur measurements, a male the Nine had never bothered to bless, but one who'd outsmarted the once great war chief when it *mattered*.

Sickle had sent an entire horde of infected lost ambling after Balkazar, and he'd done it with a song of spite and loathing burning in his Hathorian heart.

But he didn't think of the hurt. The fear that he too was infected. His wounds festering beneath the healing poultice where Balkazar's claws had marked him. Didn't think of the prince who'd died to save him or the tiny queen at the bottom of a pit. That dainty, *perfect* female doomed by the virus, chained to a titan who called himself mate.

King of the beyond.

Giaus.

No, Sickle couldn't think of them. Couldn't allow his grief to live alongside the addictive flavor of vengeance that lingered on his palate, and so he set them all aside, knowing they too would meet their end in the horde Balkazar would bring to the clearing on red stone. An ancient riverbed where a queen had been born only to die.

The stink of sulfur-born reptiles was distraction enough. A reminder that he'd claimed refuge in a place that appeared abandoned, but wouldn't stay that way for long. It was too perfect a hole. Defensible with the promise of many exits, cool and dank enough to store food without risking rot. Hidden and discreet.

It was a paradise for the vicious. Those who survived or died by the flames of the Nine, as Sickle himself had never had to do.

Until now.

But he had no tools. Nothing to protect himself from attack, and no way to hunt and fill his larders with enough to last him the winter.

All he had was a satchel of medical supplies that needed replenishing and a belly full of fumes and hatred.

He glanced at the tiny things lurking in his shadow.

The six fledglings would make a decent meal or two, but what if another brood mother moved in to replace the one who'd died so viciously outside?

What if the thing that had been her end —whatever it was—returned to claim this den?

Ears pressed flat to his skull, Sickle bared his teeth. Fists clenched at his sides.

No.

He would not die here. Not after all he'd done. All he'd seen and lost.

Pacing, distracted and trying to ignore the dull ache of his wounds, Sickle shucked his medical pack and scowled into the gloom.

Sinadim would tell him to find a weapon, an advantage over the dull, primordial brains of the predators who outranked him. Some way for him to triumph against impossible odds.

And if he couldn't find something... he'd need to *make* it.

In the absence of Anhur claws or sheer, indomitable power, Sickle had no choice but to play to his strengths.

His wit.

Qualities Balkazar—that worthless doomed relic—would insist no Hathorian possessed.

Swallowing an anxious lump peppered with spite and loathing, the Hathorian male nodded. His decision made, witnessed only by the welcoming dark and the starving things that lurked within it. The creatures who outranked him, and those he felt a pang of empathy toward.

A high-pitched coo dragged his attention into the moment.

He looked and found the female wrym. That crimson frill hidden and folded and tucked flat against her throat in such a way that she might have been mistaken for a male if it weren't for the dull spots speckling her scaly hide and the secret peek of a blood-red throat. She stood alone in her unblinking vigilance, watching Sickle through slitted glare.

Coiled in the dark, her tiny limbs braced to lunge. Neck bent and tucked tight, she trilled again, scales vibrating in a warning Sickle had only ever heard talked about, but had never seen.

"Sorry, Sultana," Sickle cooed, daring to smirk into that sinister scowl. And, stooping closer, he said, "It'll be years yet before you're large enough to burn me with your noxious spit."

As if to defy him, her frill snapped open in a crimson flare—and instead of molten vomit, she opened her jaws around a warbling tri-toned cry. One that went so much deeper than his ears, it sent his brain jiggling inside its case. The jelly of his eyes turning liquid as he staggered back with both hands pressed to flat ears. Teeth clenched hard enough to taste the scream of crackling enamel, Sickle issued a wretched shriek of his own...

... and stumbled.

Stepping badly on the uneven cave floor, he was sabotaged by an unseen crevasse. A crack in the stone that sent his ankle twisting seconds before he went down in a graceless heap of senseless, Hathorian goo. But he didn't feel the impact. Took no notice of the way his skin split when it struck a jagged rock and didn't care at all when the males returned.

He merely tried to crawl away from that piercing howl. Unfolding himself from the fetal position, he pulled his fingertips from ears that had grown tacky with blood and fled. Blind to all else, *utterly* incapacitated by a fledgling wrym who had no business wielding a weapon such as *that*, he dragged himself away.

The female fell silent.

Sickle opened his eyes and saw nothing as his brain tried to adjust to the absence. The whites of his eyes now speckled red with blood that couldn't ooze, the orbs swollen as if having suffered repeated blows to the back of his head.

Shaking, his skin slick with traumatized sweat, Sickle swiped at a trail of tacky wet that spilled from his nose and blinked as his vision cleared.

Five matching sets of vertical pupils waited. That primal hatred replaced by a look Sickle knew well, for it was one he'd seen too many times on the faces of the Anhur who'd ruled him—joy of the hunt.

An insignificant weight landed between his shoulder blades. The sixth clutchling, a tiny female with crimson frill and a voice that would send horror into the blood of the Nine themselves.

She issued one final, dainty trill...

... and commanded her siblings to dine without bothering to kill...

Waking with a jolt, soaked in sour sweat, Sinadim tried to swallow the anguish but found his throat parched. Dry and cracked where it hadn't been sliced raw.

Thirst.

It clawed at him. Ravaged and raged. Burning away any hint of sense or logic, it devoured his thoughts. Time distorting around the need to plunge his head beneath the surface of the river and drink. Deeply. Until he couldn't take another gulp.

He swallowed again and it stuck. Throat swollen and gritty, he could taste infection. Smeared across the roof of his mouth, the back of his tongue, it invaded his sinuses. Blinking, Sinadim's head lolled to the side. His fractured attention drawn by movement in the dark of their prison. The sound of boulders rolling down the side of a mountain.

Rich and heavy, it settled at the base of his

skull with weight enough to prevent him from lifting his head. Made him forget that unquenchable lust beating at the inseam of his pants, forget the thirst, if only for a moment. Urging him toward peace... submission...

But something in him rebelled.

He hated that sound, even when his own throat ached to compete. To recreate it in a way that might show the female held rapt and entranced that *he* was the better choice of mate.

Entranced by the startling display of intimacy, Sinadim stared into Renegade's blank and glossy eyes. Counting her blinks. The number of times Giaus' fingers traveled from scalp to the tangled ends of silky black hair. Sinadim made a record of every tiny, insignificant detail as the pair huddled together in the dark, soaking up the scraps of their bond. Feasting on their excess, he let another male's purr seep into his chest, where it settled and felt like the rattle of health.

And then he fell into the sleep of the aggressively ill.

Lulled by that sound. By the air vibrating between them.

The way Giaus' throat rumbled and danced, singing for Renegade as she lay boneless across his chest. Her cunt oozing slick, wasting precious moisture as she wept for that melody. The muscles of her lower back twitching... bunching in a rhythm that hinted at the purest sort of contentment. A thing that might have been displayed in the sailing arch of a flicking tail, had she such a thing to display.

Instead, she could do little more than drool.

Her eyes open but vacant. No longer shivering with the mark of ill health, Giaus' large hand was pressed to the back of her skull. Keeping one ear pressed to his chest as he uttered that perplexing drone, he petted her with the sort of careful attention Sinadim would have thought impossible after tasting the violence Giaus' was capable of inflicting.

A giant unafraid to purr for a lowly Hathorian breeder.

That sound was infectious, for Sinadim felt an answering rumble deep in his chest. A rising bubble he fought to burst, even as he was wracked with violent tremors. Plagued by the killing fever as it settled deep into his bones, aching where he couldn't scratch. Where he couldn't do much of anything but hope... watch... gorging himself on the bounty that was Giaus and his Renegade.

He slept.

And when he could manage to lift his lids once more, it was to the sight of rolling hips and stretched, pale flesh. Flesh that slid against his own in their cramped prison, for he'd lost the battle against gravity on that slippery granite floor. Feet braced against the far wall, his entire left side pressed against the blistering heat of feral muscle.

Naked and hot.

That throbbing purr played havoc with Sinadim's senses.

Overlong legs spread, Giaus' tail was pinned beneath Sinadim's calf. A detail that stuck, despite the lewd display of shameless fucking. The writhing limbs and the scent of wanting, laced with the sourness of the virus working so deep inside.

Renegade was spread and stuffed—Sinadim could see it in exquisite detail. Could reach out and touch... press against the flexing wink of her back entrance, if he were bold enough to risk his own life. Daring enough to ready her for his desperate, aching need...

His cock pulsed where it was held behind tattered laces and damp leather, a burst of seed spilling at the thought of having her like that. Of pinning Giaus beneath them both as he showed the other what it was to be a prince. Third in line to the Sultan's throne.

Helpless to stop, drunk on the fumes of so taboo a thrill, Sinadim's hand slipped down. Bumping over ribs, the ridges of taut abdominal muscles, and the point of his hips, he tore himself free. Palmed the heavy pulse beating in his cock and stroked it, *hard*. From tip to aching base, he worked his shaft and watched Renegade ride.

On top.

Her breasts swaying with the gentle rocking, Giaus let her work. Indulging her in a
manner Sinadim himself had never thought
to allow.

The fever pillaged his restraint, leaving
him pliant to his base needs.

Here, in the dark where none could see.

Where he was nothing.

Heedless of the danger Giaus posed, he
fisted his base and stopped his knot before it
swelled. Knowing just how to drag this out, to
make it last.

It seemed impossible, watching her like
that. The slow roll of her hips as she ground
herself against that dark nest of curls, her
movements not her own. She was enslaved to
that purr. Dancing at Giaus' whim, rippling
over his length. Winding ever tighter as his
song rose in pitch. And then her head fell
back. Her chin drifting to the side, she exposed her throat and submitted in a graceful
curl of sinew and muscle.

Eye contact.

It electrified him, pushing the killing
fever back. Thirst forgotten, just for a moment. Long enough that Sinadim was caught
in those empty black pools and fell in deep. A
willing victim. One fist working his length,
the other milking his knot despite the ache of
sickness chewing on his spine, he watched
Renegade come apart.

Neither blinking, until her eyes rolled
back. A soundless scream stretching her lips

wide as they might go, her every movement held precious as she shuddered around Giaus' cock. Keening... body begging for more...

He savored every second.

It wasn't the sounds that set him off. The sordid wet squelch of female flesh gushing cream as her orgasm rippled through her abdomen.

Wasn't the scent of slick screaming for him to taste and surrender to the rut. The unconscious demand that he lose himself just once more before Giaus made a wreath of his entrails.

And it wasn't that he was touching the most dangerous male he'd ever laid eyes on. Thigh to thigh with the luxurious, prickling heat of a male he was bound to.

It was the complete surrender Giaus had bought with a purr. Enslaving a creature like Renegade with so simple a trick—one he ached to try. His throat twitching around a song meant to drive her into his arms, despite that it was wrong. That there would be consequences for what he'd done. That he'd sullied the purity of the blood running through his veins.

Blood to blood to blood.

Anhur males tied together in sickness and corruption. A fallen prince and a peasant who would be king, between them, a female who dared.

Renegade.

Hathorian queen.

His queen.

His... mate.

Sinadim swallowed but didn't blink.

Balls flexing, knot blooming against his palm, he couldn't look away from those vacant, glossy pools of tepid black.

Giaus reacted.

Taking advantage of his sheer size, his overwhelming reach advantage, Giaus' fist found an anchor in her hair, and with it, he forced her to twist. Index finger hooked between her lips, Giaus set his knuckle between her teeth and made her open before he guided her down.

Chilled and wet, her tongue skipped off Sinadim's weeping prick, and so the first salty splash striped across the bridge of her nose.

"Drink," Giaus barked, purr rattling through the single syllable. Forcing obedience without a blink, he adjusted and pushed at the back of her head. Made her lips stretch around that glossy helm, and bade her swallow every lashing drop of Sinadim's seed.

"Fuck—" Toes curling, Sinadim left one hand on his knot. Jerking his base, he painted her tongue. The back of her throat. Feeding her everything he had, his fingers laced over Giaus' without a thought. Hips pumping with all the pitiful strength he could muster.

She gulped it all down, ruining him with hollow cheeks. Nursing until his balls dropped and his head hit the granite. Until the strength went out of his limbs in a rush that left him weak and shivering once more.

Shamed.

Blissfully so.

Still rumbling, Giaus reclaimed his mate. Lifting her easily, his massive hands dwarfing her waist—fingers touching where he cradled her narrow ribs—he held her aloft. Pulled her off his thick, shining cock, and set her between his legs.

It was the same process. A command to, "Drink," gentle guiding pressure, and another male filled her mouth with a few precious, meager calories and a drop of moisture.

A drink.

Hazy, delirious with thirst, Sinadim swallowed a dry, wheezing cough as Renegade's cheeks bulged around a mouthful. Her throat working to obey, pretty, sopping cunt left on display... Glistening in the dim light.

Giaus' eyes tracked his every movement. Daring him to touch.

For a moment, the Anhur stared at each other. One with bristling mane, the other trembling under the might of a killing fever.

And then, with a cocky smirk, Giaus' cock popped free of plumped lips. An audible smack splatting against the feral's stomach, he traced the bridge of Renegade's nose. Scooped up that first splash of Sinadim's seed and pushed it into her mouth.

Wasting nothing, for she came first.

Their mate.

3

Purring, Giaus' voice was distorted and raw, his vocal cords chaffed by long hours of extended effort. Savaged by the need to soothe his precious Renegade, to see her through the worst of the killing fever that had rendered her so pliant. So helpless and fragile in his arms.

All to no avail.

She was limp.

Her head lolling at grotesque angles when he tried to wake her with gentle force. And there, echoing at the back of his skull, the prince's words were there to haunt his every action. His every aborted plan and sinister intention curbed by a veiled threat, by a bluff Giaus couldn't call without also risking her life.

"You'll kill her with ignorance long before she bears your monstrous seed..."

Giaus scowled down at the other male, his slumped and tangled form no longer the stature of one who'd been a prince, Sinadim was broken. Battered and bruised, his golden flesh hidden beneath layers of vibrant blues, greens, and purples, he lay unconscious as the virus worked great change where few but Giaus himself could see it.

But most hideous of all, a mark at the base of Sinadim's throat. The delicate imprint of a Hathorian mating bite.

"She's claimed a second mate..."

No matter how much it hurt, Giaus knew it was true—it was in her scent. In the way her chin tipped toward the other male, even in her oblivion. She was hungry for Sinadim... aching for them *both*.

Behaving exactly as Sinadim had said she would.

Giaus snarled under his breath, breaking the hypnotic cadence of his purr. The tiny female in his arms twitched and frowned at the lack, squirming against the heat of his chest.

But her breathing remained shallow. Wet. Her eyes fluttering behind lids he had to pry open only to find orbs stained a bloodshot white, gleaming with a nauseating hint of yellow.

She was dying.

Succumbing to the deadly thrall of the Trax virus before his very eyes, for she was Hathorian. As precious as she was coveted, she'd been a harem breeder before he'd made her a queen. Trained to submit to her master's every depraved whim, to accommodate the needs of a predatory species not her own.

Smaller...

Weaker...

Less.

Her kind had been engineered to lift their tails and breed for the Anhur. Meant to take nothing for themselves. To whelp legions of sons who'd die for fathers who'd never learn their names, and birth hybrid daughters they'd never know. Hybrid females whose only purpose was to nurse Anhur babes and spread their sterile cunts for Anhur males not important enough to have the privilege of owning a creature like his Renegade.

His mate.

A Hathorian Omega.

"What do you know of keeping Omegas, oh mighty king of the beyond?" the prince had asked through a sneer, goading Giaus with everything he didn't know about his precious Hathorian queen. *"I know everything you've never thought to ask... every weakness and secret strength... You won't last three days without me, and for your failure, you'll suffer unimaginable agony..."*

That was the impassable threat. The blade's edge Sinadim held him to, even as he too succumbed to the Trax.

Sinadim lay there absent any hint of sense, and yet, every drop of power was hooked between the other's claws with a single ominous promise.

"She can feel everything... Mutilate me," the prince had whispered through cracked and bleeding lips, *"if you want to torture her..."*

There was no risking it. No way to test the bounds of his noose without harming the creature Giaus loved so dearly.

Or worse.

Giaus' queen, dead from neglect before she ever had a chance to step into her incredible potential.

"We're mated. Even as she milks your knot, she'll beg for mine. To deny her is a death sentence more cruel than killing her here and now... and she will *die without the attention of her mate, Giaus. And now, either of us will do..."*

Born of pure defiance, his purr rumbled back to life, and with a careful touch, Giaus ran the tips of his ruined claws through her hair. Combing through the snarls of glorious black silk made wet with sour sweat, he traced the shell of her delicate ears. Scratching at the base, he traced the cone to its pointed tip, then worked his way down. To the space between her brows, where a frown had marred that perfect skin.

"You are equal to this suffering," he murmured against her clammy skin, rubbing at the joint hidden in her hairline, where her ear was anchored to her scalp. Forcing one expressive ear to lay flat, as he'd seen her do so many times before. Her temper was a wholly unexpected thing to see in a creature so small and dainty. A temper Giaus had seen and matched, taken as direct, *delicious* challenge to his own relentless need to have her spread and submissive before him. He'd meant to watch her fall, seduced by her nature. Her tail lifted to please him.

But she'd fought him with every last scrap of might she possessed. Made him earn his place above her. Inside her.

By the Nine, how she'd rewarded him with her choice! The imprint of her teeth a wound he would worry with his claws until it festered and scarred, no matter that it was a gift he now had to share with Sinadim.

It was a treasure.

Head dipping, he pressed his nose to her hairline and took her in deep. Breathing against damp hair, his tongue flicked back to paint the roof of his mouth. To taste her in a way no other might.

Sick.

His lungs were full with a queasy breath of one edging ever closer to death.

But there was a fragile layer of something else there, too. A whisper of hope that promised great change.

Giaus could smell it—*taste* it—a secret hidden beneath a greasy film of putrid infection.

Ambrosia.

A whisper of her incredible potential, for in her tiny, fragile body, the Trax had become something new. Something that might turn the tides of these feral wars and grant Giaus an everlasting rule.

Not a Sultan, but a King.

And she was dying.

"I'll kill them all if you die, my sweet Renegade," Giaus rumbled and pressed his forehead to one that was at once tacky and dry. Too hot beneath the chill. "My precious mate."

He got no answer from her beloved lips. No sign that she could hear anything at all where she'd gone.

Heart pounding inside his massive chest, Giaus allowed himself a moment to endure the blistering panic churning in his gut. To succumb—if only for an instant—to the terrible knowledge that she might never open her eyes again.

And it was his fault.

His strain of Trax that worked to unmake her.

The very same variant that had rendered Balkazar a walking pustulence, brains all but leaking from the war chief's ears.

If such a thing were to happen to Renegade...

Giaus pulled her closer, trying to force his indomitable lust for life into her fragile body.

"More than either of us," Sinadim had whispered, forcing the words through a parched and bleeding throat, *"she needs to drink to replace what is lost in slick as she produces for two mates..."*

Giaus scowled at the other male who shared their dreary prison. The interloper who dared to touch what Giaus had claimed.

And in his frantic need to pacify her, Giaus himself had fed her what little Sinadim had to offer. Despite the way it burned in his chest, he'd turned her lips toward that pillar of flesh and bade her drink. Watching as she nursed at Sinadim's cock, seething as she gulped down a few meager swallows of brine that couldn't possibly suffice.

Not for long.

Not here, abandoned in the dark with no food or water. Forgotten at the bottom of a dreary prison with no support, no pack coming to save them from the squalor where they'd been forgotten.

Eying the ceiling of their dank pit, Giaus sneered at so flimsy a confinement. It would be nothing for him to scale the crumbling walls, to reach and dismantle the pathetic lattice keeping him contained, were he not nursing his own wounds. Tied to not one, but two ailing mates.

The word gave him pause.

Unspoken, yet profound, it echoed in the space between his brain and skull. Leaving tiny, unsettling marks deep on the surface of his very nature.

Golden, feral eyes slipped over to the other male once more. Seeing the swelling that marred Sinadim's royal features in a new gloomy light.

Mated.

Not in the same obsessively proud way Giaus bore Renegade's mark but mated nonetheless. Bound together through a female neither were worthy of, a tiny slip of a girl who might well succumb to the virus and take them both with her.

And for a moment, as he watched the former prince strain to draw breath, Giaus considered the risk of calling that bluff... to reach through the distance between them and simply... snap Sinadim's neck.

His claws extended, dimpling his palms.

From above, a shadow fell across the floor of the pit. Dust, pebbles, and a shower of loose shale pattered the tops of Giaus' shoulders, coating him in a fine ruddy layer he didn't bother to brush off. Instead, he glared at the silhouette standing high above. Eying the bulk of a hybrid male whose name he hadn't bothered to learn.

"Supper," was all the hybrid said before dropping a bundle over the edge.

Giaus extended one long forearm and snatched the package from the air. A package that rattled.

And then, in a voice dry with something that might have been shame or regret, "It's not... We couldn't hunt... sorry."

He waited, watching as the lid to their prison thumped shut once more. And when he tore into the makeshift bag, it was to find an accidental gift.

Bones.

Cooked and picked clean, only the barest whisper of meat clung to those ivory shafts.

But Giaus smiled, appeased by such a boon. For it wasn't the first time he'd almost starved, hamstrung by an injury. Weakened and in need of calories to heal.

Settling back with the sort of smirk befitting royalty, Giaus weighed the largest bone in his palm and found it solid. *Full* of marrow.

Eaten raw, it was a hard and spongy substance. A tedious chore.

But cooked?

Salvation had been dropped neatly into his pocked and ruined claws.

Not wasting another moment, Giaus cracked one of the long bones in half, careful that any spillage landed on Renegade's pale stomach. Using her as a serving platter, just so he might lick her clean. A meal enjoyed at his leisure, despite the dreary circumstances.

And then—ankles crossed, head tipped back—he set the broken edge to his lips and swallowed the buttery paste. Tongue darting out to scoop up the leftovers. He drained three entire bones like that, slurping up calories as fast as he could. Swallowing without tasting. Didn't stop until he was dizzy with the rush of nutrients and there was a mass of congealed fat sitting heavy in his gut.

Without bothering to stand and disturb his unconscious mate, Giaus took the longest of the bones and broke the bulbous knuckle clean off. Leaving only a hollow pipe drained of marrow, which he set against the smooth granite bedrock of their prison floor.

Already wet from filtered river runoff, it made the perfect whetstone. One he utilized with practiced efficiency, grinding that first bone down until he had a rough spigot.

Large enough to be used as a faucet, to tap the river's potential and quench the extreme thirst ravaging his mate's throat—a thirst that needed to be quenched, or she would never survive this hellish infection. Dead of dehydration as the slick spilled and spilled from her honeyed cunt.

Collecting the club end of the thickest of the bones, Giaus eyed the layers of shale that made up the dripping walls, set that pipe between the sheets of rock, and struck it with his makeshift hammer. Pounding it deeper until he was satisfied with the anchor and the first hint of moisture began to bead along the freshly ground edge.

Slow at first, but it wasn't long before a steady drizzle of water began to flow through the tap. Landing wasted on the floor of their prison.

Undeterred, Giaus gathered himself to use what little energy he'd gained from his meal and went to work. Measuring where the water fell, he took the heavy, blunt knuckle bone and began to hammer out a shallow pool. A reservoir that held the slightest hint scent of sulfur, but was sweet enough to save them from a long, slow desiccation.

Enough to speed his recovery and free him of this pathetic pit.

Only when the pool had filled and he'd drunk his fill did he open another of the bones. Dipping his forefinger, Giaus gazed into the pallid face of his mate and painted her lips. Teasing the tip of her tongue with the rich, buttery flavor of marrow.

She didn't react. Eyes fluttering behind lids swollen shut, Renegade was held prisoner inside her mind. Growing weaker with each rattling, watery breath.

"On... on her gums," Sinadim rasped, a rogue tear leaking from his ruined silver eye as he watched from the gloom. Roused by the sounds of construction.

Mane bristling to a stand, Giaus grunted through his teeth.

"Rub it on her gums. To start"—a violent shiver racked the fallen prince's entire body—"to start digestion."

Without taking his eyes off the other, Giaus dipped his finger anew, parted her lips with his opposite thumb, then rubbed the oily, life-saving grease over Renegade's gums. Coating the inside of her lips. Probing between her teeth, he painted her tongue in a slow lurid thrust, enticing her to suck.

She moaned, the sound a whisper of anguish that rattled against Giaus' ears. Speaking of just how far she'd fallen to the virus, how quickly. That she wouldn't persist for much longer without direct intervention.

Nursing at his finger, Renegade caught his wrist in a grip that trembled with weakness.

Sinadim hummed—a happy sound that managed to lack any hint of heat. Gloating was utterly absent in the one-eyed male. Instead, Sinadim struggled to sit. Twisting until his back was against the wall at Giaus' side, the prince heaved for breath and settled in. And then, careful of the still-weeping wounds where his claws had caught and lacerated her almost down to the bone, Sinadim draped Renegade's slender legs across his lap. Seemingly content to play second to Giaus' lead.

It was Renegade's contented sigh that saved Sinadim from a vicious death. His life preserved only because of the way her tongue searched for any missed droplet of marrow. The promise of *life* in the gentle suck and pull against the king's finger.

And through a thunderous glare, Giaus was made to watch as her tiny feet were swallowed up in big hands that weren't his own, but those of her second mate...

4

Teeth.

The prickle of needle-sharp razors that sliced through Sickle's skin as a desperate wrym took a bite. Gnawing and chewing, the fledgling squealed. Frantic, clearly frustrated. A storm of desperate need that spoke of starvation... of neglect, for their mother was dead. Her corpse a hollow shell that had given all there was to give.

Sickle hissed and spun, trying to throw his unwelcome leech before she found bone.

She only worked harder.

Trying to tear a mouthful free, evading his grasp, Sultana issued the frustrated snarl of a creature not quite strong enough to claim that chunk of flesh, despite the ominous squelch of ripping skin. The trickle of warmth as it ran down Sickle's back.

Grinding his teeth, Sickle's spine twisted as he reached over his shoulder, caught the tiny wriggling body, and hurled the female at the cave wall with a shout of victory.

It was a pale thing that didn't last.

Long and sinuous, she twisted before she fell, landing on her forefeet. Already coiled and ready for another strike when her back legs touched down. Claws skittered across stone, and with a dainty coo, her frill snapped open in a crimson flare. The female issuing a low warble in that alien voice that promised the sort of pain only the Nine might match.

As if commanded, another set of teeth latched at his nape. Another wail of panicked starvation punctuated by the thrashing of a juvenile trying to tear at living flesh.

And again at his hip.

His forearm.

Thigh.

The males jumped to do her bidding, all five attacking with teeth and claws and no small amount of vicious intention.

Arms thrown over his face, Sickle staggered to his feet. Eyes searching the gloom for something—anything—except for dust and stone and piles of stinking lizard shit.

At the far end of the tunnel, the light of an exit caught his attention, glimmering with the promise of tomorrow. And yet... the Omega male hesitated.

Balkazar would call it cowardice to flee from a worthy opponent.

Even now, Sickle could hear the vicious

mockery he'd take for choosing survival over honor.

Even in death.

His ears flicked back, jaws clicking shut to reveal the savage point of interlocking canines.

The war chief wasn't there, and only the living were afforded the luxury of shame.

Favoring his right ankle, he limped as he stumbled, swatting at the neonates hard enough to send them spinning into the dark with nothing but a taste of their meal.

All it took was another thrumming bark from their tiny queen, and they surged forward once more. Relentless. Obeying her every command, they attacked him where he was blind. Targeting where he couldn't reach, his calves and hamstrings.

"Get off!" Sickle bellowed, whirling to face the swarming lava-kin even as he continued to retreat. Flashing the points of his teeth in a warning that went unheeded. Skin flushed and wet with sweat and gore, he spun and twisted, battling the lava-kin with ever-increasing panic. To think that after everything—after exile, the virus, threats of rape, and the death of everything he'd ever known —he'd fall to a horde of baby monsters still wet with yolk and hardly out of their shells.

It was absurd.

Enough that he laughed when the panic boiled over and left his sanity a tattered wreckage. "Come on, then!" he hollered, shouting to be heard over the lingering echo of Sultana's brutal song. His ears caked with drying blood. "Work for your meal!"

Lips peeled back, Sickle planted his feet. Lower back flexing where his tail had once been, his ears pressed flat to his skull in a slick, blond arc. Ready for the coming violence.

He thought of Sinadim, then. Radiating defiance, his fingers grew damp with longing —for a blade, a club, for anything he might use as a weapon to defend himself against a wave of one of the deadliest predators lurking in the great beyond.

There was nothing but his wit. The reckless unpredictability of a creature cornered by the promise of a brutal death.

If he fell here, now, Sickle knew he'd be eaten alive. Knew no one was coming to the rescue. There was no pack of misfit brothers. No fallen prince or hated war chief.

This is what it was to be alone. To be a Hathorian and live free.

Feet braced, Sickle snarled, for there was nothing at all left to lose and no reason to cower from the end.

The males scattered before his wrath. Reforming as a group, they stood between their intended meal and their unblooded queen. Protective, lightning-fast, yet silent as they waited without blinking. Attuned to her every breath.

Sultana yipped and ordered her army forward.

Swinging and dodging, Sickle did his best to evade and ignored the lancing slice of pain when he was too slow. And when one of the males landed a strike at his forearm and won a bloody mouthful, Sickle issued a yelp of his own.

"Fuck!" he snarled and staggered back. Too slow to retaliate, he pressed his back against the wall and cornered himself. Hiding his blind spot in jagged stone.

Sharp stone.

Reaching without daring to take his eyes off the surging reptiles, Sickle scrambled to claim a weapon. Cutting his fingers, his knuckles and palm, before a shard broke free.

It was then, as he panted for breath and bled freely from a dozen wounds, that Sickle knew an instant of hope. A glimmer dangerous enough to make him reckless when he said, "Alright, Sultana. A fight to the end," he hissed, and made eye contact with the little lady commanding her army. "Let the winner eat until their belly is full."

Jaws gaping, Sultana took a breath that expanded her chest and throat. Displaying a minuscule flash of color that spoke of what she might look like as an adult, she prepared to issue another of those deadly, impossible howls.

He saw the air shimmer all around her, and before her next exhale, Sickle launched into action and charged the wall of males at a full sprint. Ignoring the slicing, snipping pain of hungry mouths, he went straight for the would-be matriarch and caught her by the throat, forcing her silence with the palm of his hand.

"I don't think so," he whispered and noticed when the males froze in place. Utterly still, five sets of gleaming reptilian eyes remained fixed not to Sickle, but to their queen and the stone blade he held against her thick hide.

Dancing back on the balls of his feet—nimble and evasive as only a Hathorian could be—Sickle held his prize aloft and flashed his teeth at the other five...

... and stabbed Sultana where her belly was soft.

The blade crumbled against her scales. Useless. A thing sharp enough to make him bleed meant nothing at all to that young queen.

An eerie, dense silence settled in the dank air.

An impasse.

But they didn't attack. None but Sultana herself dared to move.

Frowning at their lack of action, Sickle dropped his useless blade and caught Sultana's tail in his free hand when she tried to twist and whip. Instead, he tested the attention of her clutch-mates and moved her wriggling body to the left.

Five necks twisted in perfect sync.

Clutched in sweating palms, he moved Sultana to the right in a gentle, swaying arc.

Five chins tracked every millimeter of her movement.

And then he knew—when not a single one of the males blinked or flinched or moved—what the difference was between Sultana and her male counterparts. And, flexing his wrist to inspect those vertically slitted pupils, he met Sultana's eyes and crooned, "They're your thralls, aren't they? Can't sing like you do, hmm little queen?"

Seething hatred was her only response, but there was something... beautiful to be found in her alien glare. In the gentle slope of an angular brow and the neat point of her toothy muzzle.

He thought about breaking her neck, then. Impenetrable scales or not, Sickle wondered what might happen if he were to shatter the thrall she held over the males with a single sharp wrench of fragile bone. Would they attack or scatter? Unify without a queen to lead them, or strike out on their own to thrive or perish as they searched for a new queen to rule them.

Blood dripped from his elbow. Flowing free from some unseen wound to spatter on the dusty stone.

A tiny tail coiled about his thumb, weaving between his fingers.

"Back!" he barked and thrust her before

him. A threat that might ruin them all, he brandished her body as if it were a torch. Moving with purpose, he limped to the shallow crack responsible for his twisted ankle and forced the lizard queen inside. Keeping her pinned with one hand, he dragged a loose plate of shale over with the other and moved to trap her in a makeshift prison. A mirror of the one where Renegade moldered. Contained, yet breathing.

And yet... her spine was left unbent, his grip on her airway loose. Absent anything more sinister than a vague threat of harm.

It was a distant thing, the recognition that he was hesitating. That he shouldn't have named the tiny queen or spent so long staring into her gleaming yellow eyes. That perhaps, just maybe, she'd enthralled him too.

"I'm not *that* desperate to serve a new queen," he murmured and secured the roof of Sultana's prison with a heavier boulder.

He wasn't entirely sure what it was he intended to do with the wryms. Didn't know if he meant that prison to be a larder or a stable, but he stepped back all the same. Hands hanging loose at his sides, ready for whichever path the males might take, he watched the remaining siblings swarm forward. Their cries grew ever more frantic as they tried in vain to free her, to push a rock that to them was a bolder.

Delirious, bleeding and raw, Sickle stumbled for that exit. Haunted by the cries of juvenile lizards only half as real as the ghosts whispering insults that occupied his every waking thought.

It was madness to let them live. To take the risk for something as pathetic as sentiment, for creatures who felt only spite that he'd managed to escape with only a few ounces of flesh paid.

Renegade was dead.

His loyalty to the prince absolved.

Lust for vengeance satisfied by Balkazar, who'd deserved it most.

Only Giaus had escaped the bulk of the consequences, but what did it matter, really? Who was Giaus to him, but the catalyst of the end that was already written the moment they'd been exiled.

If not Giaus, a horde.

Or the Trax.

Or a rampaging predator stronger and faster and ultimately more deadly than even the most brutal Anhur—anything hardy enough to survive the wilds might be the thing to end them.

There was poetry in knowing some part of it had been Renegade. An Omega female, one of *his* people. Glorious to the end.

But ended she was.

To mourn her by giving up was pitiful.

An insult to an Omega who'd have been equal to any Anhur queen Sickle had ever served.

Clinging to stone walls, he pressed on. Not quite sure where he was going, he knew only what he left behind.

A life lived for others. One he'd meant to reclaim before it was over.

But the fragile thing he'd been... that pathetic creature who'd known only to cower in the shadow of Anhur masters?

He'd perished in the dark alongside the prince who'd tried to save him... expired with the queen he'd loved at the hands of a king he'd loathed.

Sickle was gone.

Covered in dust and blood, he stepped into the light of early dawn. A shadow that hardly bothered to move, he inched forward on silent feet—and found himself before a smoking carcass. All that remained of a giant, the brood mother had been all but picked clean. He could see it in the way her scales sagged around a void. Hollowed out from the inside, they'd gone in through her eyes. Slipped down her gullet and eaten her tongue.

With a grimace, he inched forward and peered into the face of death. Those gaping, unhinged jaws lined with row upon row of teeth blackened by her very nature.

He reached. Touched the pointed tip and bloodied his finger for his trouble. "Sharp as obsidian," he whispered and smeared a streak of crimson between forefinger and thumb.

An idea took root. One born of blood and bruises, in open wounds and stinking lizard shit. It was as unhinged as what remained of the brood mother's jaw, and yet, it was a new start. Crazy enough to gain the attention and respect of the Nine, if ever they'd bother to look at a lowly Hathorian male.

All he had to do was take it. Fight or die by his own hand.

As Renegade would have done.

Sickle could never do such a thing...

... but who was he really, but a shade of his former self...

5

"Drink."

Blinking, his eyes gritty behind the lid, Sinadim jolted at the sound of that gruff voice. His one-eyed gaze snapping to the other male who'd saved them just so they might suffer another day.

Giaus.

The mutant king he'd agreed to serve in this new kingdom in the beyond. Second in command, a general of the feral army, for it wouldn't be long now. Not long at all before Sinadim succumbed to the virus and became a mutant himself. No longer a prince, he was among the doomed. Already he could feel it, the ache of deep, fundamental change as the virus worked to unmake him.

Infected.

Brows knit by a frown, Sinadim swallowed and tasted rot. Fingers flexing around the tiny feet cradled in his palms, his claws dimpled that delicate, female skin. She was a precious creature that made his cock ache only half as much as he ached to reject her, to take it all back and reclaim his rightful place in the Silver City.

But Giaus had saved them—provided food from nothing but a few meager table scraps. Bone marrow and running, liquid water with a bit of clever work, and an intellect the king had no right to possess.

Sinadim snorted, mane bristling, his every inhale thick with a sticky, cloying aroma that clogged his sinuses all the way to the back. Each stinking breath a dense, nauseating cloud that stuck when he swallowed.

Something rancid had died in his mouth, surely. Something that left a putrid flavor coating his tongue with a rancid film of mossy growth.

It was tacky.

Wet and... *gooey*.

"Drink," Giaus said again and pressed a cup made from bone into Sinadim's hand.

"It'll help, will it?" Sinadim asked through a sneer. But in spite of himself, he released those dainty little feet and obeyed. Head tipped back, he opened his throat and choked down a few meager swallows that would buy him time.

Time to rot, forgotten down here in the dark. Waiting for his brains to leak from his ears, for his bones to shift and break beneath the weight of grotesque growths wrought by the Trax.

He's seen it all before. Too many times to count.

"I'm dying, then?" he slurred through lips both swollen and cracked.

But to this, Giaus merely shrugged. Coy as he pulled the girl closer. The tint of feral gold caught what little light there was, only to throw the darkest shadows across their prison. And with a twitch of his lips, Giaus pressed Renegade to his chest and robbed Sinadim of her touch, all in one slick motion.

"Keep your secrets, miner," Sinadim said, and swiped at the greasy sweat beaded on his brow. Eyes falling shut on the heels of a violent shiver that sent his mane into a full, accidental flare. "But grant no mercy to the infected unworthy..."

Oblivion claimed him, then. Flinging him back into a time he hadn't remembered to mourn as he shivered and quaked. Miserable with the onset of the end.

"It's the killing fever, boy. Burns like ice, doesn't it? Like coals under the skin."

It did. Sinadim shivered again, back twisting to ease a pain too deep to touch.

"It's a poison," his father had said. *"A punishment for those who dare to defy the Nine and their gift of pure, Anhur blood. And for the insult, the infected will be left to rot from the inside out. Look,"* his father crooned and made Sinadim obey with the tip of one hooked claw. *"See her there? Your precious renegade Omega? It's only*

been hours, but already she succumbs. Pathetic creature."*

She was there in the dark... the only female who'd laid a claim on his royal skin... *the only other one to survive the attack of the hoard, though she'd been... savaged by the wave. Her tiny body battered by mindless greed and ravenous hunger.*

"No," Sinadim rasped, sightless, staring off into the gloom as fat, burning tears slid down grimy cheeks.

A callous blow struck the back of his head. "Stop your sniveling, and look! See what you've allowed to happen? This is the price, boy. You wear her mark with such pride," *Hadim spat, sneering through clenched teeth.* "Now watch her succumb, and know you might have saved her this final agony."

Frozen in place, Sinadim could do nothing but obey. Watching her skin grow lumpy and distorted, festering as if coals had been tucked beneath her skin and left to bubble and boil. One arm hung limp where the bone had been mangled and broken. A veritable club, it dangled heavy and grotesque from her delicate frame. Fingers swollen, ruined and standing stiff from a palm that was little more than a balloon of flesh.

She was ruined. Utterly. Completely.

A sob splintered over his lips as he watched the limb mutate and grow.

Lost, pitiful and abandoned, she ambled back and forth at the gates of the Silver City. Pacing a ragged line, wordlessly crying for help, until her eyes ticked up. Brown, laced with green. Her gaze was deep, hazy with confusion.

But when she found Sinadim's teary gaze, she wailed low and long. Reaching with the hand not mangled by the Trax.

The one she could lift.

"Sina!"

"Let this be a lesson," his father said and turned to go. Two fingers raised, Hadim looked to the guards at the wall. "Grant no mercy to the infected unworthy, boy."

Sina watched as the guards took aim, but he didn't cry when the spears began to fall...

Soaked in sweat, gagging, Sinadim jolted awake. Choking on the horror still mocking him behind eyes squeezed firmly shut. But despite the flood of bile, he pressed a fist to his good eye and worked to separate past from present. To divorce fevered hallucination from hopeless reality.

For if Renegade was ruined... her muscle and bone disfigured as he'd seen so many times before...

He shuddered, mane bristling, claws dimpling damp palms.

And for a moment, he was distracted from the thirst. His attention pulled away from the slicing anguish of a throat left ravaged by infection, by the need to plunge his head beneath the surface of the river and drink it down to the silt.

Distracted long enough to realize an altogether different need rode him now.

The claws of addiction had burrowed deep. Here, in the dark where his willpower had crumbled away to nothing and left him starving for a taste.

Slick.

It was a monstrous craving fit for one with royal blood, one who'd been born into outrageous privilege. And it returned with a rush that made his head spin and his cock weep. *Aching* to set his knot in a quality Omega and make up for every hour he'd been without his harem, as only a Sultan's son might.

Cracking his good eye, Sinadim dared to look. Squinting through the fog of delirium—through the blurred veil clouding his vision—he tried to catch a glimpse of the female haunting his every waking thought.

She was waiting there in the dark.

A queen dancing in silhouette. Beckoning him to sink deeper into the fog.

Her sinuous form writhing across thick, male thighs, she called to him from her perch. Begging to be knotted. Her pretty, weeping cunt creamy with want as she sheathed herself over and over and over again. Stretched to the limit where she was stuffed full by another male...

Cast in exquisite detail, she was perfection despite the blurry edges. Every sinful inch a symphony for the senses. Whole and without corruption.

The mere sight triggered his knot to swell, no matter that it was laced with something...

else. Something sour and wrong and oh so terribly dangerous.

Groaning, Sinadim squeezed his eyes shut once more. Cock pulsing where it was exposed to damp air, he gushed in answer to her call. A salty prequel he ached to bury inside that sweet, Omega warmth, even as she was spread across another.

A beast who let her ride as Sinadim himself had never thought to do.

On top.

Pert little nipples jerking in a lewd display of female dominance, he indulged himself in the taboo. Watching a phantom twirl in the dark, where none could see his secret want.

He didn't blink until the ravenous dark sucked him back under and left him senseless. Head heavy where it lay against unforgiving granite damp with a carpet of slime and algae, he floated in a tepid mist. Oblivious, until a vicious headache bloomed behind his eyes and sent little poison barbs into the jelly. Shattering the rich illusion he wasn't sure had ever been real.

"Fuck," he whispered because it was the sort of headache he knew. One he'd recognize under any circumstance without the need to question.

His addiction.

It would be worse this time, he could feel it. And, shifting to ease the ache of desiccated kidneys shriveled by fever, he twisted against the heat of another. His lower back tight with pain that had no outlet... his cock stiff with the sort of need that would get him killed, given just who he shared this prison with.

Despite the dancing queen, his working eye cracked open to look upon the beast.

Crossed at the ankle, long, powerful legs stretched out before him, Giaus appeared to sleep. His head tipped back, resting against a wall of loose shale.

A trap.

Sinadim recognized the pose of one who knew what it was to fight for survival, who knew the danger of sleep and had learned to exist without. Not quite awake, but neither was he truly at rest. It was just there, evident in the tension humming in broad shoulders. In the spread of white knuckles that were folded tight around a tiny figure.

Renegade.

The mere sight of her—there in the flesh, alive and whole—all but sent Sinadim into a savage rut. Laces already pulled loose, his cock already exposed, he shuddered as he stared. Unblinking. His eyes growing dry, he swallowed and this time it was sour.

A warning.

Throat parched in such a way that could only be soothed by *one* thing, Sinadim lifted one trembling hand and clawed at his face. At the wounds left by his father, scratching until his fingers came away wet.

She was his punishment, this girl. An illusion that couldn't be trusted, one that still wore his father's mark. He'd seen it etched in an elegant line down her back. The twisting script of her lineage written for all to see.

A brand of ownership, the mark of her worth.

Shivering, his mane bristled. Pupils blown wide only to shrink down to tiny pricks of feverish madness.

There'd be no mercy for the unworthy. The infected...

She was infected—he'd seen it. Those desolate cries still echoed in his ears, and with every blink, he could see the way she'd begun to fester. Rotting from the inside out...

Sinadim tore his bleary gaze away from the girl, head spinning with confusion and desperate need, for he might have spared her this final indignity. It was his duty.

Grant no mercy...

But what would it hurt if he had just a taste?

A quick, stolen gulp of ambrosia before the girl ran dry. Before she went out of season and left him in the crippling pain of withdrawal with no harem to supplement the lack.

Before she succumbed, and the spears began to fall...

Scratching at his face, Sinadim let his head fall back to thump against a rough-hewn wall. Dizzy, his vision began to blur, dancing with a spectacular array of colors and shapes that crawled beneath his skin and began to boil.

Fingers trailing down his cheek, his claws skipped over hard edges, tracing the length of his throat—and caught on a wound.

Still oozing and tender.

Fresh.

A half-moon that shouldn't be.

Sweat bloomed across his brow as he remembered.

Renegade.

Her teeth at his nape. Salvation in surrender, she'd doomed him with that deadly kiss of teeth and blood.

Claimed.

Mated.

To a fucking Omega female, one he was expected to share with a beast.

Laughter, dry and reedy, crackled over Sinadim's lips, for he finally understood.

This was to be his punishment, to die this way. He, who'd waded through the vile underbelly of Anhur society and punished the skin traders who dealt in slick. He, who'd exterminated whole nests of wretched, broken creatures bound to Anhur males who could never complete their bond, and would never grant so much as an ounce of affection.

There was no reason to ration her slick. No cause to deny his indulgence—not now. She'd given as much as she'd taken, their Hathorian queen.

Their mate.

It was a death sentence. For her. For Giaus.

Death for all three, this was payment for allowing her to mark his royal skin. For tainting the noble bloodlines and claiming a female who was *not* Anhur.

A taboo used only by the skin traders, he'd seen the horrific consequences of forcing Omegas to lay claim to an Anhur.

Their wretched pleas haunted his dreams. Mocked him with the way they'd tried to entice, begging to be mounted, desperate for the males who'd doomed them. Females who needed no season to produce slick at an alarming rate, for only a bonded Omega could produce on a whim.

And now he was no better than the lowest of the filth.

And Renegade...

Bile splashed against the back of Sinadim's throat.

Acid laced with the scent of what he wanted so badly, but couldn't stomach.

Tongue flicking out and back, he painted the roof of his mouth—and recoiled. Shocked.

All around him, the gloom ignited.

An impossible array of colors, his vision was saturated with a detailed spectrum of things that couldn't possibly be real. The dark came alive, held in a relief so stark, so painfully vivid he could almost see what he could taste. Each element held separate, illuminated with a distinct shimmering color best seen from the edge of his vision.

The killing fever. Flourishing out of control, it surged to the fore in an unstoppable wave.

Sinadim swiped at a bead of sweat before it ran into his eye, trembling with the effort. The stink of sickness lingered on his every breath, staining the air with a dense cloud of sour bile.

"Orange," he murmured, the sound a reedy hiss of agony over parched vocal cords. Lifting one shaking hand, claws hooked to grab, he tried to touch the tendril of color in the dark and sent ripples dancing across still air. Swirling in a cloud of scent that couldn't possibly be real. "Hallucination," he whispered as the ache of fever burrowed deep. Lancing through muscle and bone, twisting through too many injuries to bother counting. And there, at the back of his eyes, the pounding beat of a brain swollen by the virus.

Too often he'd seen this horror unfold.

Sending one curved claw into his ear, Sinadim's mane grew stiff with the reek of terror. That he should succumb as Balkazar had. Stinking of death, brain leaking from his ears as the virus pillaged...

But his claw came away clean.

And on his next breath, he caught the scent of something sweet laced with a hint of rich grease.

Marrow. Savory and just a touch rancid, it

held the promise of life in a stack of charred bone.

His tongue flicked back once more, gliding over subtle pits that lined the roof of his mouth in parallel strips. Obeying some bizarre new instinct that demanded he smear saliva against the pits—and for his obedience, a heady flavor exploded behind his sinuses. One he knew well, though he'd never seen it through the lens of fevered hallucination.

Slick.

A pool of liquid gold had spilled from that honeyed pot. Soaking Giaus' lap with an ambrosia worthy of the Nine themselves, Renegade wept for them. Producing coveted nectar out of season, she beckoned to him even through her misery. Engineered to present for her master, just as he'd been born to mount a breeding Omega and stuff her full of his knot. His sperm sealed tight inside until that seed took root.

Danger utterly forgotten, Sinadim shifted toward his female. Toward the slit drooling for his knot.

Blind to the danger wrapped all around her, he licked at that shimmering, golden trail hanging thick in the air. Slipping and sliding toward his prize as the rut settled into his veins, he approached the sleeping giant who'd bade him drink...

A tiny sip couldn't hurt...

6

Sprinting as fast as he was able, the war chief fled from certain death. Lumbering and crashing through the brush, passing trees that danced and shimmered with colors impossible to describe, he worked to out-pace the horde. Hounded by the thunder of a thousand footfalls, he ran with an uneven gait. His left foot heavier than the other, he moved with a distinct *thump-pat* that made stealth impossible.

Balkazar's hunting days were over. An era at its end, for in place of a calm, steady mind, there was corruption. Rot. Decay that filled him with false confidence and lifted the burden of logic from his uneven shoulders.

His was a brain swollen by infection, riddled with abscesses and pustules.

Vision off kilter where one ear was tipped toward the earth, Balkazar swiped at the goo streaming from his nostrils. Heaving for breath through gaping jaws.

Thump-pat, thump-pat.

A wet snarl burst from his lips, and without bothering to look, Balkazar lashed out at the trunk of a sapling, cutting it down with a single easy swipe even as he trudged forward.

They mocked his progress, the trees. Standing in the way of his mad flight—forcing him to dodge and weave—they whispered things he couldn't quite hear. That he should turn back. Join with the legion and serve it from within so he might feed the beast what it was owed...

Balkazar shivered as he ran.

Murmured lies, all of 'em. Tripe that distracted from the one and only thing that truly mattered.

Sinadim.

It was the only clear thought present in Balkazar's rotten mind. The distant drone of the horde, the demands of the many spoken in a language he had no interest in learning... all of it was overpowered by thoughts of his prince. Thoughts that echoed in the puss that leaked from his ears, in his every faltering footfall as he fled the horde.

He had to get back to the pack.

Couldn't rest until he'd returned to that clearing of red stone, where the end had begun. Where the least of them had been given the first taste and an Omega female had named herself queen.

All of it for nothing if Balkazar failed.

Sinadim had to be warned.

The prince must be made aware of the coming wave before it crashed over them. Had to know just who'd sent it to drown them all, if only so he might warn the Nine of the betrayer in their midst and stop him from returning.

Sickle.

Insolent little shit.

He'd slipped away before Balkazar could take him to task. Abandoned his oath to the brotherhood with weepy little tears staining his face, and for *what*?

That sodden fucking quim, that's what. Betraying his brothers for a meager sip of Hathorian slick, for a few spoken words from a female who'd been just as happy to present any of her holes to a beast as a prince. Her cunt open to any male willing to shove his prick inside and leave it messier than he'd found it.

She couldn't help it, he knew. Hers was a meaningless life lived in service to her betters. Property with a simple purpose—to breed for a prince and feed their addiction to slick. It was what she'd done for Hadim before he'd thrown her out and left her ruined. Docked and mutilated like the rest of them, she was bred for temptation, the lure that had brought them a gift meant for a prince.

Sneering, Balkazar's mane flared in an uneven halo about his shoulders. Three claws on his left hand shot out, catching at the trunk of a mighty oak as he barreled past.

Thump-pat, thump-pat.

And Sickle had thrown everything away for nothing more than the tainted fucking memory of the little bitch. Even now, she belonged to another. If the beast hadn't ruined her with his absurd girth, she'd be stuffed full of the prince's knot. Begging for more, as she was trained to do. It was her purpose, her destiny to bear the first litter born to the wilds.

Everything was as it should be.

Everything in the proper place, falling into the specific order willed and written by the Nine themselves...

... until Sickle had refused his duties. Pouting because he thought himself above his station. That *he* should be the one to be mated to Renegade.

A grin spread over the war chief's cracked and flaking lips. Lips that were swollen and disfigured on the left side, lumpy and hard where they should have been soft.

The boy would pay for his crimes to the pack, Balkazar would see to it himself. Such was his duty when Sinadim himself was occupied.

He sniffed back a glob of phlegm and stumbled to a halt. Pausing his flight to fish his prick from his pants, the war chief set his forearm to a tree whose trunk seemed the most stable and aimed at the roots.

Little shit thought Balkazar was a relic?

Spittle dribbled down his chin.

Insolent brat.

Sickle would regret all he'd said. All he'd done in her name. As soon as Sinadim rose up from the dark, Balkazar could resume the hunt and recover his honor. With his prince at his side, the war chief would swear a new oath. To defend a new line, one who'd inherit the majesty of a gift not meant for the likes of Giaus or Renegade.

The Trax had been for Sinadim.

It had *always* been for Sinadim.

Thumb pressing into soft flesh, the war chief scowled down at his cock. Making the slit pop open with a squeeze that quickly became brutal, that sensitive glands flushed purple in the vice of a clawed fist.

But not a drop of piss dribbled out.

"Needs a legacccy," he mumbled and horked up a wad of slime as he stuffed himself back behind his leathers. "A quality bitch with Anhur blood. Not some"—a shiver rattled down the bumps of his spine—"some… Hathorian slag shitting out half-breed sons."

At his back, the low drone of the horde trickled through the trees. Approaching in a relentless wave, they moaned in a single voice that lulled him into distraction. Made his grotesque head turn toward the sound as they drew ever nearer, listening as they seemed to call out his name. One he didn't recognize as his, but was meant for him all the same.

An uneven halo flared up around Balkazar's shoulders. It was instinct. Some almost forgotten trepidation that warned him to flee, and with his head tipped back, the war chief caught the breeze through a tiny open hole in clogged sinuses. Scent sticking to the goop of infection, he lumbered toward the whiff of familiar males. Every step bringing him closer to his prince.

Thump-pat, thump-pat.

Hobbling as fast as he could, Balkazar stumbled through a forest swirling with vibrant colors and fantastical creatures. Trees whose trunks wriggled and danced, only to snap back into rigid uniformity the instant he looked. A metallic sheen coated everything—from the chaotic half-truths wriggling before his eyes to the taste laying thick on his pallet.

Blood and gold and copper that was green and pink.

A hysterical giggle burst from uneven lips, and throwing his hands out to the sides, Balkazar roared. Bringing the sound up all the way from the bottom of soggy lungs.

He'd had no idea!

Never felt so alive or seen such color in the world.

Swinging his left arm, Balkazar obliterated the trunk of a purple tree trunk. Sending a shower of gleaming silver wood to litter the earth as he ambled by, he pounded at his chest—aggravating the wounds left by Sinadim's claws. Wounds that had already healed over with a crust of flesh that was easily twice as thick as it had been before.

Balkazar clawed at the ridges and sucked back a glob of snot to clear his airway. The scars were a gift, he knew. Armor, given to him by his prince, who awaited him in the shadows of the Nine themselves. A prince who'd disowned him too soon, who didn't yet know what it was Balkazar had given him.

But he'd learn.

Adjusting his course, the war chief followed his nose to the edge of a quiet creek that was laced with the barest whispered hint of slick.

Renegade.

Mane spiking up, he bristled at the memory of a female who would dare. Defiant, she'd stood before a prince without fear and without lineage, issuing orders as if she was anything more than what she'd been born to be.

An incubator for cannon fodder. A womb with legs and perfumed cunt.

The memory sent a surge of blood to bloat his cock, and with glassy eyes, Balkazar clawed at his prick. Shredding his leathers as he trudged through the deepest part of the creek.

Oh, he'd have another taste. He'd lap up whatever spilled cream the prince deigned to share, then cram a few hybrids into her belly that would grow strong and hale beside royal blood.

Fisting himself below the water's surface, Balkazar shuddered as an overeager drop burst from his tip, and took no notice of a spurt tinged an alarming shade of crimson...

When Sinadim rose up from the dark, a fiery crown on his brow, Balkazar would ask his reward. To breed the girl in the old ways, witnessed by the pack, beneath the watchful gaze of the triplet moons.

He cleared the creek and fell to his knees, stumbling on dry ground. Unable to adapt to the change in terrain, he dragged a few precious sips of oxygen into swampy lungs.

And for a moment, as colors became smells and the sounds of the wood grew to be insidious whispers, he was lost. Head spinning, brain swollen and threatening to spill from his ears, Balkazar was serenaded by the voice of the legion. Drawn back the way he'd come, where a thousand shuffling feet marched on his sloppy trail...

Sinadim.

One eye green, the other silver, he was radiance itself. Pure-blooded, a direct descendant of the Nine, even before Balkazar had given him to the dark where his fate lurked in fetid shadows.

A smile creased a face that had become grotesque, that grew more disproportionate with every lurching twitch of infected muscle. The only recognizable feature of an Anhur male that had once been known as Balkazar was the distinct shade of piercing blue eyes, now laced with murky gleaming bronze...

"You'll ssseee, brother..." he slurred, and wobbled to his feet. Watery eyes rolling until they caught on an expanse of dusty, red stone. "You'll seeeee..."

The slopes of an ancient riverbed, now nothing more than a gently burbling creek. Ringed on three sides by dense forest, it was a clearing backed by a sheer cliff face. One the infected male recognized, from somewhere deeper than the puss and rot.

With claws fully extended, growing at an uneven pace on his left hand, he ambled toward the mouth of a cave. Head tipped back to catch the scent of any who might yet linger in that cursed clearing...

Brain filled with insidious whispers. Murmurings that mocked his progress for the futile attempt it had become, for there was no denying the tsunami surging at his back. The ravenous maw of the many who knew.

He'd turn back.

He'd join the horde and become a servant to the legion...

Because the beast was *so hungry*...

7

Giaus' eyes snapped open, his mane bristling in a full flare before he'd so much as taken a breath.

The dark was alive—he felt it move and shift around him where he couldn't see. Heavy with an ominous presence violating the deep silence of their prison.

He blinked. Vision slow to adjust even as his fingers grew tight on the slender female draped across his lap. And, in a single breath, the king of the beyond shifted from rest into readiness. A deadly monstrosity that would defend what was his and take no issue with dealing death on a whim.

A curtain of dense silence hung heavy in the gloom. Silence that breathed, watching with all the ravenous stillness of a raptor on the hunt.

Lips parting, Giaus' tongue flicked out, pulling a breath between his teeth, he painted the roof of his mouth and tasted the damp mist seething before him...

... then smiled.

This was no true threat. Nothing he wasn't uniquely prepared to deal with, for he was king of a newborn species. He alone knew what it was to conquer the wilds, and with an arrogant flick of his tail, Giaus readied himself to pluck a mewling baby monster from the gloom.

Muscles coiled, he was still.

Appearing vulnerable to all who dared venture close enough to look.

Senses honed to a needle point, he suppressed the flare of his mane. Willed his heart rate to slow, his pheromones muted as he pulled another breath through lax lips.

Closer...

Giaus exhaled, pupils blown wide as they might go. Gobbling up every speck of available light, using his every unnatural advantage, his breath was steady in his chest even as he prepared himself for an explosion of muscle and violence.

At his elbow, the steady *drip, drip, drip* of water trickled from the end of the spigot, framing the fall of tiny stones as they tumbled down from the rim of the pit.

And just there, cradled in arms meant for murder, dainty, ragged breaths puffed and whistled through the dark—Renegade. His queen. He could tell by the weight of each breath. By the movement against his palms and the wet clatter that trembled in her fragile chest.

But there was another lurking in the dark.

The slow glide of his claws—pocked and ruined from his battle with the brood mother —slid from their sheaths. Fully extended. Still deadly...

Ready.

In an instant, the gloom snarled and lunged—going in for the killing blow.

With a twitch that didn't so much as disturb his precious mate, Giaus' free hand shot out and found purchase around something that was soft. Fist cinching tight and unforgiving around a column of blood and bones he ached to crush into a fine paste, but didn't.

Couldn't.

"Sinadim," he drawled instead. A droll greeting as he shifted Renegade from his lap to the ground and hefted the fallen prince into a shaft of gloomy light so he could see what kind of monster he'd caught. Claws toying with the other male's airway, he dimpled skin where arteries strained for free passage. "Still with us, general?" he asked, tone light and breezy despite the way the other choked and thrashed.

For a moment, the only response was a wet, hacking cough scarcely able to eek through Giaus' fingers. And with the gentle press of his thumb beneath the prince's chin, Giaus looked to answer his own question—

and turned Sinadim's face so it might reflect what little light there was.

Gone was the cultured face of a male born to obscene privilege. In its place, a savage. Snarling and thrashing, a fine mist of spittle fogged Giaus' cheeks as the other fought for breath that wasn't given. A damp film that bore all the scent markers he'd been waiting to taste on Renegade.

Trax.

No longer the sour, toxic thing thriving in his own blood, this was a new strain. Stable. Born of horror the likes of which Sinadim couldn't comprehend, it was a whisper of change hanging thick in the still air. A lineage Giaus had paid dearly to pass down, a pedigree harboring the potential for greatness and horror in equal measure.

Only time would tell which sat before him now.

Issuing a breathless howl of mad defiance, Sinadim clawed at Giaus' wrist and left deep gouges in the king's forearm. Lacerations Giaus ignored in favor of careful inspection.

Where the prince had been beaten and bruised, he was now nearly without blemish. Any injuries he'd earned were no longer obvious points of weakness to be exploited, his damaged shoulder working in sync with the other. The quiet crunch of cracked ribs was no longer audible with Sinadim's every breath.

But there was no recognition on the other's face.

Only a disappointing madness Giaus had seen too many times before.

"Do I have to put you down, sweet prince?" he hummed, musing aloud as he adjusted his grip and pinned Sinadim to the loose shale by his throat. Content to watch a vein bulge at the other male's temple, enjoying the sight of his claws where they left shadowed dimples. Lusting after the thought of extinguishing his rival, aching to spill Sinadim's blood, he traced that bulging vein with his thumb and let his claw drag at tender skin.

Blinking, Sinadim's eyes cracked open. "Didn't"—he choked—"didn't take you for suicidal, miner," he spat.

Droll amusement bubbled from between Giaus' lips, and with a careful touch, he pried Sinadim's left eyelid all the way open to see what gleamed beneath. "I was a smith," he reminded, absentmindedly.

It was there. Bright tendrils laced through an eye that had once been a vibrant green, and now held something... *more.*

Gold.

The same shade Giaus had seen in his own reflection now glared back at him from the prince's working eye.

Evidence of one undeniable truth.

Sinadim had survived the killing fever—a

fever that still held Renegade in deadly, merciless claws.

He couldn't help but send a forlorn glance back. Down. To look upon the delicate features of the female he'd risked everything to claim. A female he couldn't bear to lose, but one he may have killed all the same.

Lashing out, Sinadim took advantage of the lapse in attention and kicked, trying to catch Giaus high between his legs. Straining to free himself, his eyes rolled and he too found where Renegade lay in the dark. Limp, helpless, and yet, the heady scent of battle-ready pheromones rose up between them as the prince reached for the female they *both* called mate. Sinadim's mane a full, shivering flare of uncontrolled, sweat-damp fur that warned of his willingness to fight for the right to rut their queen.

To die for breeding rights.

And so Giaus asked again, "Are you with me, general?" His tone mocking and cruel, his smile one that was only half as cutting as the claws that dimpled the prince's throat.

"Give her to me!" Sinadim bellowed, spittle spraying over his lips. "She is *death*," he spat and coughed until his face purpled and Giaus was made to loosen his grip or watch him strangle. "Let me taste my doom," he gasped and clawed at his scars. Opening old wounds, even as the Trax worked to close them.

And then, without so much as blinking,

Sinadim's head tipped back. His chin jutting out, toward Renegade, and Giaus watched the prince draw a breath through parted lips. Watched him paint her scent along the roof of his mouth—and knew.

He no longer stood alone as *other*.

"What do you see?" Giaus asked, tone a hypnotic lure meant to entice.

"Gold," Sinadim breathed without missing a beat. "Liquid, honeyed gold spilling from her cunt. It's *mine*," he howled, thrashing anew. "My birthright! My punishment! Give her to me! She dances for *me*"—he retched but didn't slow—"begs for my knot. I *need* it," he rasped, ranting but more lucid with every passing moment. "Let me quench my thirst and drown in a river of slick before she runs dry... before... before the spears fall..."

Giaus' head tipped to the side, and a simple, placid, "No," was his only response.

Kicking again, Sinadim's back arched and thumped hard against the wall. Easily restrained, he was forced to pause when Giaus' forearm found his throat. A shudder rippled through Sinadim's muscle, chattering between his molars, but still, he snarled, "She's *mine*!"

Surging into action with an ease that should have warned Sinadim of the danger, but didn't, Giaus flipped the fallen prince around. Broke his eye contact with Renegade's limp almost-corpse, and made him face the wall. "You think to take her from me, boy? That you can?"

"I will have your bones torn from your shins!" Sinadim howled. "Stripped free of muscle if only so I might stuff your loose meat with hot coals and the coveted Karahmet blend of mirr and *enmote*. Spiced to perfection," he spat. "The nerves will be left intact so you can feel it"—a barking cough that was both dry and bubbling—"so you can feel your final meal as it cooks past medium rare. So it kills the parasites writhing in your filthy commoner blood—"

The air shivered with warning an instant too late.

Pausing only to mash his royal cheek into the cutting edge of loose shale, Giaus hauled one arm behind Sinadim's back and wrenched that wrist high between his shoulder blades. Not stopping until bone ground against cartilage and he was rewarded by an involuntary hiss of pain—only then did Giaus kick Sinadim's ankles wide as they might go. Grinding the other into the stone with the press of his hips, his weight leveraged against Sinadim's hamstrings. His lower back.

All of it done in one slick, merciless motion.

Grotesque and hideous, it was poetry. An art performed by a master of carnage, a symphony sung in the whine of ligaments stretching too far, in the knuckle of a joint made to roll *almost* out of place.

His claws prickled a warning deep inside that royal, sweat-damp armpit. The perfect place to loose a dozen tendons all at once. And then, pressing his nose behind Sinadim's ear, where his scent was thickest... rich and un-tainted, Giaus took a breath that rattled and whispered, "Think you can do it with one arm?"

On a blink, Sinadim's one-eyed gaze rolled back over his shoulder to find Giaus' face. Awareness seemed to shimmer behind the sheen of madness for just a moment. "I'm dying," he rasped and dragged a wet breath into his lungs. "Give her to me once before I spill from my ears, you feral cunt."

Giaus' laugh was a cruel sneer of rejec-tion, and he asked again, "Tell me what you see."

Taking a steadying breath, Sinadim worked to focus. His gaze roamed over Giaus' features before his lids fluttered shut, before his chin tilted back and he pulled a breath through his teeth. Filtering the damp air, forcing it to whistle along the roof of his mouth.

"She dances in the dark," he whispered and licked at the air. Wetting his lips before his tongue flicked back to paint his palate once more. "I can see her... draped in tendrils of floating, swirling gold as it spills from that honeyed slit." He shivered, mane bristling for an instant before flattening out. "It's not real. A ha-hallucination."

It was Giaus' turn to take a rattling breath, to force so-called honeyed air to whistle over his dimpled palate... his eyes drifting closed so he could really *look*.

It was exactly as Sinadim said.

Renegade lay in a pool of gleaming ambrosia, her every breath a plume of swirling enticement Giaus could taste. Every faceted detail of her poor health was spelled out in the twisting eddies of laced air.

Exactly as she'd been the instant he'd first caught her scent in that laced river water. Too diluted to do more than entice, but enough to draw him in from afar and command him to abandon everything he'd worked to gain.

But it was not his precious mate who'd captured Giaus' attention. Not the realization that another shared his sixth sense, or that Renegade had done what he'd hoped she might.

It was the curious whisper of a male in rut.

A male who hadn't had so much as a taste of their mate, but who was lost in the throes of a savage rut all the same.

Sweating through what remained of his shirt, Sinadim's skin was cool and clammy. His fever broken, despite his claims of delirious hallucination.

Pulling another rattling breath through his teeth, Giaus inhaled. Breathing deep, just so he could feel it when the other male cringed, he pressed Sinadim's blind eye against their prison wall and ground a bulging threat against the prince's tail stump.

Arousal surged through his blood. Brought on by the scent of his queen, but a convenient weapon nevertheless. His unnatural heat was a subtle threat laid down an instant before he hiked Sinadim's wrist higher, forcing him to stand on the balls of his toes or suffer a dislocated joint.

Before he issued a generous compromise. "Everything you do to her," Giaus drawled and made sure the other male could feel his intention, "I will do to you."

A half-strangled sob sputtered over Sinadim's lips, but that was all.

Cold, barking laughter burst from Giaus' lips. "You're thinking about it, aren't you, general?"

Sinadim's free hand thumped against the wall, his claws leaving deep furrows in stone as he snarled, "You don't know what it's like! The addiction! I cannot stop. I'll do heinous things to sate this agony. Things I went to war to end. Things I've done a thousand times in my mind since she put these cursed marks on my flesh!"

Eyes narrowed, Giaus frowned. At the tone, at the desperate, vulnerable edge that lacked all sense of cutting humor. "Explain."

For a moment, there was nothing but the sound of heavy breathing. The patter of falling stone and trickling water. Two males trapped together in an uneasy alliance, neither making an effort to disguise their desire for spilled blood.

And then, "You've never tasted it, have you?"

Giaus' silence was answer enough.

"Do everything you can," Sinadim said through bitter laughter, twisting so he might see their mate once more. "Everything in your power to abstain, or she will enslave you just as soundly. I *need* it," Sinadim whispered. "Slick. To be so close…" He shook his head, mane bristling against Giaus' knuckles—and there, in the subtle arch of his lower back… the prince pressed against Giaus in a way that drew lewd, taboo interest. "I can't… can't help myself."

A sneer tugged at Giaus' lip, and he forced, "You'd risk her life for it?" through clenched teeth. "Even now, as she hovers on the edge of death? Knowing she could never handle the rut in her current state?"

Sinadim shuddered. "Even then," he replied. "It's in the air. Gold *everywhere*." He whined, mane fully risen, his pheromones broadcast in a direct challenge to the king's claim. "I can't stop. Don't care what it costs, or that it won't be long before I join Balkazar in foaming madness," he breathed and met Giaus' glare with one that was crazed. Rimmed in white. "I'll do anything, pay *anything* for just one more taste…"

"Who is this Balkazar, and why has he got your royal ball bag in such a mighty twist?" Giaus asked instead, distracting Sinadim from his heated perusal of Renegade's still form.

"My war chief," Sinadim said and offered a watery smirk. "The one who gave you that little love tap oozing between your ribs, if I recall correctly."

Giaus chuckled and released his deadly grip, only to soften his touch. Stepping back. "Ah," he hummed and scooped Renegade back into his arms. "The shitrag. A male who threw you into the dark to suffer my mercy."

"The very same," Sinadim spat and slid down the wall. Watching with that wary, one-eyed gaze that gleamed in the dark. "But let me offer you advice before I join him in ruin, and my brains begin to ooze from my ears—"

The king rolled his eyes, tired of the mis-truth. "You are not my creation."

Confused silence echoed between them, and Giaus was content to wait. To allow Sinadim to draw his own conclusions, what-ever they may be.

But then the prince's wide, shocked gaze fell to Renegade, and with his fingers pal-pating that hated, crescent moon bleeding high on his shoulder, he said, "*She* infected me."

"Yes," Giaus hummed because there was no use in a general ignorant of his own lin-eage. "It would seem that in her, the virus has become something with less of a tumultuous nature. In Balkazar, doom," he sneered. "But in her? Well..." A smile creased his lips, and carding his claws through strands of silky black, Giaus took a moment to admire her fine, elegant features. "Something else."

"A new strain," Sinadim whispered, as if afraid of who might hear it. Awed, even as he tipped his head back and pulled a breath between his teeth. Testing his new sense with an altogether different perspective. "Mutations that are stable... Giaus. Do you know what this means?"

The king flicked an arrogant sneer at his general. "If she succumbs," he said and left the worst of it unsaid. "If she fails to thrive and never opens her eyes again, there will be no kingdom. No feral army to march on your precious Silver City. I will kill you all and the Nine themselves will tremble at my feet."

For a long while, Sinadim let the threat shiver in the impenetrable gloom. Saying nothing as he watched the king with his queen. He held the rut at bay through sheer force of will and tasted their interactions, testing the depths of his blooming gifts, where the sensory pits had formed along the roof of his mouth.

And then, "I have known hundreds of Omegas," Sinadim murmured, scratching at his silver eye, at terrible scars that no longer wept or oozed. "Tasted a thousand more. But none of them have been *her*. She will wake," he said and offered a tight, crooked smile. Confident in the way of the truly ignorant. "Because she is equal to this suffering. *My Liege.*"

Giaus couldn't help the flash of teeth, nor the grin that split his face wide open.

It was a fragile moment shared between enemies.

One destined to shatter, for it couldn't last. Their private bubble was doomed to burst.

From above, chaos. The desperate shouting of males in need of leadership.

From below, the rumble of a thousand footfalls.

"What in the name of the Nine"—Sinadim staggered to his feet, claws extended, mane standing on end. His rut muted by the only thing that could truly distract him from the clutches of his rut.

War.

Giaus alone remained. His jaw tight. His scowl deep as his grip threatened to grow cruel where it was wrapped around tender skin. Only one word spilled from his lips. An explanation and a proclamation all in one.

"Horde."

8

Sinadim blinked, staring down at Giaus for just a moment. Just long enough for that word to settle into his skull and take root.

A horde.

"By the Nine..."

The rumble of a thousand marching feet drummed a warning that trembled in Sinadim's spinal fluid. Felt in the small of his back, where his severed tail flicked an agitated, unseen rhythm. Where the ghosts of his youth wailed for mercy as they were swallowed in a single, greedy gulp.

"We have to get out," Sinadim breathed, testing limbs now miraculously free of injury. Limbs that surged with the promise of a strength he'd never known before and couldn't test at the bottom of a pit. "We can fortify the cave," he said, lucid with the rush of panic pounding in his chest. "Block the entrance, if we've got the time. Spears, if we don't." He scanned the shear wall in search of a way out. "Even then, it may not be enough. The hybrids... *Sickle*... They'll be slaughtered if we can't escape."

Giaus hummed, but that was all.

Whirling, Sinadim scowled down at the mutant. "You'd let them die?"

"I'd let them live," the giant countered and shrugged. "If they're worthy of it."

A chill rippled through Sinadim's mane, his jaw hanging slack as he looked upon the male who dared to call himself king—and wouldn't act. "Giaus..." Sinadim shook his head. "You'd let them die for nothing. You'd be king of *nothing*. For what?"

Eerie, luminous eyes flicked up to meet Sinadim's scowl. Eyes that gleamed feral gold laced with sinister amusement, reflecting what little light there was.

"Have you forgotten?" Giaus asked and tucked Renegade's pale, limp form deeper into the crook of one massive arm.

"Forgotten *what*?"

"Where were they," the king drawled, "when Balkazar beat you into submission and threw you into the dark? Where were your precious hybrids," he asked and didn't blink, "when you were left here to die with no food or water? Beaten to the edge of death. Exposed to a virus that produces horrors that drove an entire civilization into hiding?" Bristling, Giaus let his mane flare, his scent broadcasting his derision with far more precision than any sneer ever could. "They left you to *rot*, dear prince, and they are unworthy of saving."

"It's our blood pact," Sinadim said, defensive of his brethren despite the horrible ring of truth in Giaus' bitter words. Swallowing even as a muscle jumped at the corner of his jaw. "Grant no mercy to the hopeless infected."

"And yet"—claws flicking through the gloom, Giaus gestured at his massive, mutant self—"here I am. Alive, at your mercy."

A shout of alarm echoed in the distance, muffled through the layers of rock.

"They're good men," Sinadim pressed, looking up. Fists clenched as he tried to suppress the flare of his mane. To master himself and win this point. His instinct screaming that Giaus alone could stop it. "Valuable warriors."

"They *were*," Giaus drawled, and offered a horrible toothy grin. "How do you know they haven't been infected while you slept at the bottom of a pit?"

Cold sweat bloomed along the back of Sinadim's nape, where his mane stood on full, bristling end.

Balkazar. There hadn't been time to warn the others before...

"You're toying with me," Sinadim said, attention snared by the way Giaus' smirk curled at the edges. By the twinkling, amber gleam of a gaze half hidden. Watching from beneath lowered lashes. "Micha's instincts are unparalleled."

That amber glare dropped, once more inspecting the exotic sweep of Hathorian bone structure. "Then they will survive the horde and prove themselves worthy of a place in my kingdom. Or they will die," Giaus said, careless. Cold and indifferent, even while his touch was delicate on Renegade's cheek. Her brow. "Forgotten," he murmured, and one massive hand dropped to the cradle between her hips. "Easily replaced."

"You're a fool," Sinadim hissed and took a single menacing step—before Giaus stopped him with a glare. "Micha, Keever and Konjo —they're blooded warriors—"

"Loyal to *you*, if they've any loyalty at all. Tell me," Giaus drawled, and inspected his ruined claws. "Why would I want such fickle creatures in my court? Even as servants."

Sinadim scoffed. "Hybrids are loyal to their fathers until their fathers fall and free them in death or exile." He clawed at his scars, itching at a wound that was no longer oozing but itched all the same. "And then? They're mercenaries who serve any Anhur worthy of their skill. Who'd serve *you*, if—"

"*Your* men."

A frustrated snarl burst free of Sinadim's lips. "Why would you want them dead? We have a real chance to build something here! This... this queen's landing—it's defensible! Guarded at the rear by a wall of stone, a river on one side, forest everywhere else. We've got resources and comfort for the first time since our exile from the Silver City. But we cannot hold this place and guard the girl without soldiers to stand between us and a horde!"

That infuriating little smirk returned to crease the king's lips. "What the horde needs," he said, "is something to chase." Giaus lifted one burly shoulder, and said, "They have their use—as bait."

"So that's it?" Sinadim asked, clawing at his cheek. "Am I to be a general of nothing in your kingdom of the dead? You'd rather it be just the three of us? Running. Enduring the wilds and the predators and the next horde and the next. Constantly struggling to defend her until one of us dies, or she falls pregnant with hybrids who cannot carry your line forward." He laughed. Bitter. Reckless. "You cannot be a king without a throne or legacy, Giaus."

Eyes slitted to a dangerous margin, Giaus' mane flared and his scent grew heavy in the still air. "Speak your next words very carefully, little prince."

But it was far too late for caution. "Sickle is with them!" Sinadim shouted. "In him, the ability to produce more Hathorians. More hybrids. And the potential for us to break my bond with the girl, so you might have her all to yourself!"

"At the cost of breeding my mate to yet another of *your* men?"

"Sickle is *hers*," Sinadim countered, swiping at the anxious sweat beading along his brow. "Hathorian males serve their queens—and no other." It was Sinadim's turn to sneer, and in doing so, he condemned the Omega male and his matronly heart. "The little fool is in *love*. With nothing more than a few words and a single sloppy fuck, she took his heart."

At this, Giaus threw his head back and laughed. Ignoring yet another round of panicked shouting as it grew closer and the window for aid grew more narrow by the second. "I should feed you a fist full of your own jaundiced liver."

"These are the choices of sultans," Sinadim snapped. Fists clenched at his sides, his mane flared into a full bristling halo reeking of defiance. Of challenge. "Difficult, uncomfortable decisions I was born to make. My experience won by surviving a vicious hellscape of sibling rivalry that earned me the title of First Born. You want a general for your feral army?"

Giaus hummed, one brow cocked. Smirk firmly in place as he combed through the wild snarls of fine, black silk.

"Then heed my expert fucking counsel. To have a matching set of *healthy* Hathorians, out here? Where an Omega female is only slightly more valuable than an Omega male? And *her*?" he said, chin jutting an instant before he gestured at himself. "This new strain that doesn't kill but grants divine sight? *Giaus* —the Nine themselves are speaking to us! Save my men from the horde," Sinadim pressed. "Save Sickle, and let us see what can come of this feral court."

For a long moment, it seemed that Sinadim's words had fallen on deaf ears. That Giaus couldn't be moved into action that risked his life or his mate.

But with one final lingering glance, the mutant king hefted Renegade off his lap. Tucked her neatly away with her limbs all folded around herself, and stood, saying simply, "Fine." Clapping his hands clean, he turned that golden gaze up, to the latched roof of their prison. "Then let us spill some blood, shall we?"

Deflating with his shallow victory, Sinadim glanced at Renegade, mouth watering at the sight of all that naked, unguarded skin. "I *could* stay," he said and felt the rut surge to the fore. "To protect her..."

Huffing out a laugh, Giaus caught Sinadim by his ruined jacket—and tossed him like so much trash. Sent him sailing straight up in a display of sheer, unmatched strength that rendered Sinadim silent when he might have screamed.

He crashed into the lattice an instant before Giaus' bulk followed him up. Launching himself free of confinement in a single leap, the king caught Sinadim's wrist and dragged him over the ledge and straight into freedom.

"That easy, was it?" Sinadim asked, panting with the shock. With the fever that still danced inside his skull, dizzy as he balanced on the edge of an abyss where Renegade lay in peaceful ignorance. Unguarded... "If it was so easy to escape, why stay?"

At this, Giaus merely grinned—and shoved him toward the light. "To war, general."

Shaking his head, Sinadim forced his fractured mind to focus. Set the shock aside and turned his thoughts to an unwinnable battle. To the logistics of what he might find outside the shelter of this doomed bubble...

"Wait," Sinadim whispered on the heels of a gruesome thought, twisting so he might see Giaus' face and know if the other male had devious intentions. "What will you do?"

The king reeked of smug confidence when he shrugged, and said, "Slaughter the infected."

"But—"

"They cannot be saved."

"Balkazar is *your* creation," Sinadim argued, trying to force the king to slow before an apocalypse was loosed on his small pack. "Surely—"

"Balkazar will be called to join the horde if he hasn't already joined it," Giaus said, his voice a hard line that brooked no argument and sent a chill to whistle through Sinadim's blood. "Your war chief—and all hope for any others he may have infected along the way—

is gone. These are the hard truths of *kings*, Sinadim. The feral court is not your genteel Silver City. Here, death is the *only* mercy for the hopeless lost."

"And who are you to decide who lives or dies?" Sinadim snarled, tripping only for Giaus to catch him by the nape and set him right.

At this, Giaus rolled his eyes and stopped in the center of the den. Feet spread shoulder width apart, he tipped his head back and drew a breath between parted lips. "Can you not taste it?" he asked. "The corruption and rot—it's all that remains of that vile cretin you so loved."

Almost against his will, as if given permission to acknowledge what he'd won by vanquishing the killing fever, Sinadim's eyes fluttered closed. A breath pulled in. Sent swirling over the shallow dimples now lining the roof of his mouth, where scents became tastes he could see.

The explosion of color was just as jarring as it had been the first time. Just as bewildering to his overwrought mind.

"Pick one trail," Giaus hummed. "Tease it free of the others."

Sweat beaded across Sinadim's brow, rolling down the deep furrow of scars that no longer itched or wept.

They were dancing all around him. A miasma of color and texture indiscernible from one to the next—until he did as Giaus said.

It was there, all around him. The evidence of daily pack life was a rich, storied narrative he could unravel with a single breath.

He could see it all.

The phantom of his fight with Balkazar, painted in angry swirls of noxious fumes. The pattern of violence disturbed by Sickle's passing as the Omega had fled certain death, and again by Micha—who'd been the one to deliver a pitiful bundle of charred bones.

With a single flick of his tongue, Sinadim knew Keever and Konjo had come no closer than the mouth of the den.

He had the taste of their fear.

And just there, hidden where only he and Giaus might see, thin, imperceptible tendrils of golden slick buried beneath mundane layers.

But he knew, without a hint of doubt, that none of them showed any signs of infection. None but Balkazar.

Rotten from blood to bone with a strain of Trax that offered nothing but misery.

"The things I can see," he whispered, staggering toward the light. Incredulous and dazed as his feet moved and his brain spun.

From the clearing, a roar. That of a beast in pain, it jarred Sinadim into action and banished any trace of miraculous sight. In an instant, his vision cleared to show the drab, dingy interior of Renegade's den, and any hint of fantastic color receded back, into the shadows from where it had come.

It was a roar he recognized, distorted though it may be.

A battle cry he'd heard a thousand times, both in the Silver City and beyond it.

That of a male who'd sworn to lay down his life in protection of Sinadim's bloodline—only to betray everything he'd ever upheld as precious, for he was lost to the madness of a virus wreaking havoc in his blood and brain.

"By the Nine..."

The beast roared again, clearer now that Sinadim had stumbled closer. Drawn in by the sound that had once been a signal for attack.

It wasn't until he stood at the mouth of the den—sweat a thin, damp film laying heavy on his brow—that Sinadim saw the hard, unavoidable truth. That he understood what Giaus meant.

They cannot be saved.

Balkazar could not be saved.

Hemmed in on three sides by hybrid soldiers with spears, Balkazar was cornered. Micha stood before the fallen war chief, all broad shoulders and hard lines. "To the river," he snarled, tight and commanding. "Force him into the river!"

It was a command Balkazar himself had issued more than once. A tactic that would see a single, roaming infected slaughtered through disadvantage alone—but would be utterly meaningless against the weight of an entire horde.

A horde whose approach could not be felt above the ground.

Muscles writhing beneath his skin, Balkazar lashed out. Slow and lumbering, he swung the arm that had become a veritable club and missed. Throwing himself off balance with a howl of frustration that became an agonized wail when Keever darted in close and scored first blood.

"Don't let him touch you," Konjo warned, mirroring his twin as he too struck out and tried to force the war chief to take another step toward his doom.

Balkazar whirled toward the voice...

... and vomit scalded the back of Sinadim's throat.

An abomination stood below him. Wearing the skin of his fallen war chief—and wearing it *badly*. Twitching, grotesque, any hint of glorious Anhur beauty was gone. Swallowed by a living horror. Blue eyes bulged from their sockets, twice the size of anything that might have been considered normal. Pupils alternating between a blank, dead stare lost in some distant void, only to shrink into tiny pinpricks of intense focus an instant later. Reacting to movement, as if he was little more than a hungry mouth on a dull, vicious predator.

Revolted, Sinadim retreated a step—his back bumping against a wall of muscle and rippling testosterone.

"Easy," the king cautioned. His voice

calm. Rich and soothing, no matter the way it was laced with an eager lust for blood.

Sinadim couldn't so much as blink. Couldn't tear his eyes from the thing Balkazar had become in so short a time.

Fetid slime had soaked his chest with ropey strings of drool that dropped all the way to the top of his belt, swinging and shivering with his every erratic movement. And with every lurching twitch of muscle that bulged and shrank from one second to the next, he seemed to shimmer. A hulking monstrosity that existed in the gray, where life had not quite given way to death.

As he watched, Balkazar's head tipped back and to the left. Jaws hanging slack, the beast drew in a breath. Oblivious to the gore spilling down his thigh from the twin wounds, his misshapen head rolled on a neck far too brittle to support so lopsided a weight. His skull deformed where bone had grown out of control. Where skin was stretched too thin and swollen, all at once.

A thick, wormy tongue flicked back, painting the roof of his mouth, and Balkazar moaned in an eerie dual tone that sent alarm bristling through Sinadim's blood. And with an audible *crack*, Balkazar's neck snapped back. *Up.* Pupils dilating and constricting in an uneven pulse, his eyes wild, he searched for only a moment. Just long enough to scan the clearing before he found Sinadim where he stood before the king.

And then three things happened all at once.

Balkazar fell to his knees with a sound that might have been jubilant, his mouth working around a string of garbled nonsense. "*'Mpiiince! Ahworrd!*"

As one, all three hybrid males reeled back, spears poised to fall. To put him out of his misery, and grant the infected war chief this one final mercy.

And from the trees, the voice of a legion. Groaning, the army of the lost began to burst through the trees. A trickle that would become a flood.

It was then, as Sinadim watched a dozen bodies become a score, that Balkazar's jumbled words condensed, his meaning as obvious as it was poetic. Full circle.

"*My prince!*" he'd said. "*A horde.*"

<h1 style="text-align:center">9</h1>

They came through the trees.

Slowed by the trunks large enough to forbid great speed, the infected trickled onto the battlefield. One by one. Some lumbered under the weight of ghastly mutations, others newly infected. Smaller, weaker, but much faster.

The first wave, Giaus knew.

One of many.

Shouts of alarm rose from Sinadim's hybrids, and the twins fell back, behind the largest male whose dark hide was covered in thick, raised scars. Their names were irrelevant to the king watching them retreat as a cohesive unit, as they backed toward the cave with spears at the ready. Utterly outnumbered.

Standing there stark naked, Giaus stretched the kink in his ribs where a spear had once threatened his life, golden feral gaze fixed not on the approaching tide of carnage, but to the face of the male responsible for all of it.

Balkazar the Unworthy.

He'd brought the horde to their sanctuary and threatened Renegade while she battled the killing fever—to make no mention of his attempt on Giaus' life.

The king sneered.

His head would be the prize Giaus would take for quelling this uprising in Renegade's name. A gift to his queen, the war chief reduced to a skull stripped of meat, dipped in molten iron, and mounted on the footstool of his throne—so he might always keep the unworthy lech underfoot.

Where he belonged.

Cracking his neck, Giaus' lips grew taut around a sneer, for he was whole. He had suffered Balkazar's best and come through it without so much as a scar. Healed from a wound he hadn't bothered to tend, gone before it could fester. A wound that had really only annoyed Renegade, because of the mystical bond they now shared.

His mane flared, hot and possessive. Unrestricted by clothing, the malted scent of musk rose from heated skin as a deadly surge of hormones polluted his blood. Hoppy and spiced, it was a warning as nuanced as it was subtle. That of a male willing to obliterate an army in defense of his female, so he might dress her in cured hides and bathe her in the blood of vanquished enemies. Cherished, even here.

"By the Nine," Sinadim breathed, and Giaus caught the wisp of something similar rising from the other's skin. A hated reminder that Renegade was not his alone. That although it would bring Giaus a sadistic glee to watch him struck down by the horde, the prince was just as important as the queen.

"Don't fret, sweet prince," Giaus drawled, craning his neck to leer down at his counterpart. "I'll teach you to be a warrior worthy of the feral court."

Sinadim jeered around a slitted glare. "Fuck off," he snapped, but the scent of fear rose in a bitter cloud about his shoulders. "We're outnumbered twenty to one."

"Oh, it's far more than that." And through a grim smile and clenched teeth, he shook out his hands and ordered Sinadim to, "Tell your precious hybrids to guard my mate with their worthless fucking lives."

"And how exactly," Sinadim asked, "do you think we will defeat a horde without their help?"

"*We* won't." It was then, as he watched the killing field fill with fodder, that Giaus felt something deadly creep across his face. Something that might have been a smile, but wasn't. Something starving for carnage, a darkness desperate to be unleashed in Renegade's name.

A statement would be made.

A warning to the one watching from a distance, through a thousand sets of eyes...

Below them, past the swirling pools of heated water, Balkazar lumbered away from the onslaught. Following his former pack brothers in retreat, the beast was slow. Clumsy and bumbling, yet still resisting the call of the legion Giaus himself was all too familiar with.

Curious...

"If it's your plan to fight alone, I won't stop you," Sinadim said, keeping tight to Giaus' shadow. "But what, exactly, would you like me to do while you commit suicide, *my Liege?*"

Again, Giaus was made to look upon Sinadim's scarred face with something approaching respect. An unbidden smile crinkled his lips when he snatched up a discarded spear and said, "It's your job to clean up my mess, general. Impress me."

Pressing the spear into Sinadim's hands, Giaus turned. Dick swinging in the breeze, he paid no mind to the orders shouted at his back, over his shoulders. Orders that made three bewildered sets of eyes whirl as the hybrids hesitated to obey Sinadim's commands, shocked as they were to see both of their prisoners free of confinement.

There was nothing in Giaus' mind but a swirling pallet of color. A detailed catalog of the tools he'd use to paint a masterpiece in gore, one he'd etch into the very stone beneath his feet so his deeds here today would never be forgotten.

Foregoing any illusion of stealth, Giaus filled his lungs with the breath of the Nine and bellowed his challenge. His dominance. Ownership of everything he could see—defiance of his blood and the lineage he worked so very hard to deny.

The horde moaned back. A brainless entity that moved with a single mind, they filtered through the trees from all three sides. Groaning and gurgling, they clogged up the clearing with the stink of rot. Putrid, messy beasts too stupid to know the scent of danger, they charged after the hybrids. Swarmed around Balkazar, claiming him as one of their own, they shielded Giaus' prized skull in a barrier of numbers. Hunting at the command of another, they moved as one toward the mouth of the cave.

Toward Renegade.

Giaus' claws slid free of their sheaths, and without looking back, he charged into the fray. Barreling past hybrids only too happy to avoid this battle, he flew. Faster and faster, until the stone trembled beneath his feet and the Nine themselves would surely be tempted to ascend from their burning thrones to watch all that came next.

He met the first wave with arms spread wide. Ruined claws extended in a deadly hooked net, he laughed with the pure Anhur joy of honest battle.

Colliding with a newly infected thing, Giaus' claws flashed through flesh. Catching at something vital that gushed when he tore it free and rolled easily into the next. Shifting his weight from his hips to his shoulders in a beautiful arc, he conserved strength. Tossed aside his second victim in favor of the third.

The fourth and fifth.

Moving with ever greater speed as his muscles warmed to the task. Skin flushed as his blood heated, and his senses spilled over. Honed to a tiny prick of awareness, Giaus pulled a breath through his teeth and melted into an altogether different sort of killing fever as his vision splintered and the color bled through.

The flash of a spear split through his peripherals, and without so much as a whisper of sound, Sinadim landed a mortal blow. "I presume this is what you meant by clean up?"

Giaus could only grin before he found another anchor for his deadly grip. Tossing the almost-corpse at Sinadim's feet, he moved on to the next.

And the next.

And the next, spinning and whirling, he aimed for bellies and throats. Tore at all that was vulnerable and left it ruined, his wake a river of blood and bits and slippery pits. The footing grew dangerous when he brought both hands down atop a grotesque skull— and broke the first of his claws in bone that had grown brittle with disease.

He lost three more relieving a mutant of its lower jaw—swollen, diseased tongue left wriggling where it dangled, hanging nearly untethered from a sucking maw.

Another claw crumbled when he caught a swinging fist so badly mutated it may as well have been a club.

But when teeth sliced through his right shoulder, Giaus' roar threatened to split the very wind from the earth.

His mark.

The most precious gift he'd ever been given—where Renegade had left her claim— was almost obliterated by the bite of a mindless beast.

He reached back, caught an eye socket with his forefinger, and swapped it for a digit still tipped with a deadly hook. Pressing through anything that squelched, popped, or squirted, he rotated his wrist until he heard a yelp of pain and the beast went rigid. A spasm of muscle and loose bowels were the only hint that it was death's weight growing heavy on his back.

Delighted by the swift vengeance, Giaus caught a small one by the throat and sacrificed another claw to show his captured pack brothers exactly the sort of monster he'd become...

... and obliterated that windpipe in the heart of a single deadly fist.

Decapitated, still twitching, the corpse fell at his feet in a crimson puddle already inches deep. The severed skull reduced to nothing more than housing for a set of rolling eyeballs and gnashing teeth Giaus held by the splintered edges of a crushed spine.

He was so *terribly* far from finished.

Free hand darting out, Giaus caught another beast by his open, gaping mouth—and shoved that still blinking skull between jaws wrenched unnaturally wide. Leaving it to choke without offering the courtesy to check if it was really dead before he disemboweled six more in rapid succession.

It was then, when the king spilled the belly of another into the ever-widening pool of gore, that he noticed a particular shade of cerulean blue laced with feral gold. Eyes in a face he hated well enough to take notice when their owner darted through the mayhem.

Mutated, but still lucid enough, Balkazar appeared before him. Covered in carnage, reaching not for Giaus, but Sinadim. "*'Mpii-ince!*" the beast moaned, blue eyes darting. Pupils blown wide as they might go. "*Sickle—*"

Raising one foot, tail standing stiff and tall to offer a measure of counterbalance, Giaus kicked him back and turned again. Sending his elbow to crumple one breastplate and another, attention already having moved to the next target. And the one after that. Watching as Sinadim made swift work of any who survived his wrath. He left Renegade's second mate to deal with his scraps—none of them in any sort of condition to harm the interloper he hated but couldn't kill.

The last of his claws went with a splintering pain when it was torn free from the root. Lost behind a boney protuberance he hadn't bothered to inspect before it was rendered unrecognizable in his fist. Pulped where it wasn't dangling and jagged.

"Giaus!"

Alarm ringing loud enough to capture his attention, the king turned toward the sound.

Sinadim. Spattered in crimson, cheeks sallow, he yanked his spear from a twitching body—and jerked his chin in the opposite direction.

The second wave was upon them.

Older mutants that had survived battles and brutal winters, dense hides littered with scars and protruding bone that had left them little more than lumberous, armored tanks. They were dense creatures all but unable to walk on two feet, relegated to all fours with the weight of their deformations.

A true behemoth trundled through the trees, moving on balled fists, on knuckles that had flattened to something more closely resembling cloven hooves.

Notoriously hard to kill, they were a living shield that would allow smaller, more agile infected to penetrate the sanctuary where Renegade slumbered. Where she could be spirited away while he labored to dig her out.

Giaus sprinted into the mess without a moment's hesitation. Leaving Sinadim unguarded, he went to his knees still carrying a great speed—sliding through a small ocean of blood, it was as if, just for a moment, he'd been given wings. Horrible, sticky things reeking of iron and bile, his feathers carried him forward on the winds of death. His pinions the very breath of disease.

It was pure Anhur joy.

Laughing, he threw a punch that sailed through the abdomen of a beast and seized a fist full of slippery entrails. Guts that were a length of pulsing blue and purplish rope for which he had a gruesome task in mind.

Heel catching at an outcropping of red stone, Giaus was launched to his feet once more—a trailing length of ribbon sailing in his wake, he leapt onto the back of that boney tank. Careful not to tear his macabre cable, he dragged the poor doomed creature along with him. Serenaded by the dull lowing of chattel in pain.

In seconds, he was on the other side of the tank—darted beneath its forelimbs with fluttering entrails flapping in the breeze.

He caught the disemboweled beast as he made a second pass, spun it around—as if winding a bobbin of slippery guts—and leapt over the tank's shoulder once more.

The tether ran short.

With a jolt that took the smaller beast off its feet and left it swinging madly from a torn belly, Giaus hauled back on his leash and rigged a garrote to strangle the tank with the dead, thrashing weight of another.

A counterbalance that dragged the tank toward a smothering, even as it strained to free itself.

Afforded the luxury to turn away, to conserve strength as he dove back into the writhing masses, Giaus turned just in time to see a mortal blow swing through Sinadim's blind spot.

And there was nothing he could do, but watch. Horrified by the implication—delighted by the twist of fate that might see Sinadim's bluff called, that might see his bond with Renegade severed. For better or worse.

Balkazar.

Haunting his prince's shadow, the fallen war chief caught that death strike before it could land and took the damage upon himself. Bellowing a wordless protest, Balkazar swung back, his claws leaving horror in their wake.

Something howled back.

Something *big*.

A creature born of nightmares only Giaus himself had seen, it was a demon of the third wave.

One he was utterly unprepared to deal with here, now. With a vulnerable mate, and a half-blind prince tied to his every decision.

Blue eyes laced with gold flashed up to meet Giaus' stare.

And for a moment, the king saw the ugly side of his lineage in a kinder light. One that could fight the call of the legion, and *win*, for with something that might have been a tight-lipped smile stretched over ghastly gums, Balkazar's misshapen head tipped down. His chin dipping in a nod.

Solemn when he turned, drew in a lung full of righteous fury, and roared.

Loud enough that silence fell in the aftermath. That every mutated head turned toward him, muddy eyes tracking the source.

Again, Balkazar trumpeted challenge, defiance of the horde and the legion that meant to claim them all in service of a monster.

And then, with a final, lingering glance back, Balkazar the Unworthy did something that should have been impossible.

He turned heel and fled.

The horde turned with him.

Mindless. Endlessly hungry, they were drawn away from the queen's landing by a moving target. A final gesture from a decaying brain, it was sacrifice. An apology of action.

It was *love*.

"Huh," Giaus hummed, head tilting to the side. "Bait."

The earth rumbled long after the horde had turned, the heavy waves yet unseen as they clung to darkness and obscure shadow.

Their dead abandoned without a thought, their corpses left to poison any carrion eaters foolish or hungry enough to take the risk.

Straightening, Giaus clapped sticky hands and rubbed the slaughter off on his naked thighs—only for his palms to come away wetter than they'd been a moment before.

Sinadim staggered toward the behemoth still choking as it gasped and thrashed for breath, sending a lance clear through its brain he delivered mercy with the point of a spear. Only then did he move to Giaus' side. Panting. Painted in unspeakable grime, but whole. His hide undamaged, except where Renegade's mark lay upon his skin. "Fuck," he whispered, but that was all. His eyes wide as he surveyed the damage Giaus had wrought with such frightening ease.

Looking toward the void where Balkazar had been and gone.

But Giaus spared nothing for the curiosity that was the Unworthy wretch, instead, he spread his arms. Flaunting his nudity, he turned to address the hybrids standing shocked at the mouth of Renegade's den.

"Are you not impressed?" he asked, voice booming through the silence. Mane risen to display his prowess in all its magnificent, un-clothed glory. Reeking of powerful pheromones that left no question as to who had won the day. "Are you not grateful?"

As one, the twins assumed a defensive po-sition. Ready for battle they hadn't a hope of winning. Straining not to be claimed by the feral court, they stood between Giaus and his mate.

There was no deadlier place in all the wilds, tamed or not.

Head tossed back, Giaus issued a cruel bark of laughter. "You dare? This is my kingdom!" he snarled, and his voice bounced back at him. Distorted and powerful. "Your lives are already forfeit. Mine to do with as I please, for I have saved you from the legion!"

A steadying hand landed on Giaus' shoulder, where a wound wept and nearly ruined a coveted ring of scars. "This is not the Trax of old, my brothers," Sinadim said from behind. Standing on Giaus' left—where the prince was most vulnerable. His blind spot was left exposed to the king's whims, not to place Giaus on his right, but rather as a subtle gesture of trust. To submit his greatest weakness to the other male, Sinadim's blind spot was exposed. "It's..." Sinadim took a breath. Painted the roof of his mouth with the storied scents whirling around the clearing. "It's a leap of faith. One I wouldn't ask of you if the reward wasn't worth the risks."

"You ask us to die," one twin said.

"To willingly accept infection," said the other.

"I'm asking you to join me," Sinadim returned and took a step. "To submit to the feral court. To Giaus and this new variant of the virus. I'm asking for your trust, so we might rise as something new. Together."

"I've been like you," Giaus rumbled, tail lashing as he paced, pinning each of them with his alien glare. "Wandered the wilds like you. I was lost like you. But I alone have communed with the ghosts of the ancients. I was left to traverse the magma fields without the safety of pack or brothers. It wasn't one lunar cycle before I was infected," he said, mane bristling as his tail lashed. Leaving so very much unsaid. "In me, the virus became something new. A variant splintered away from the original. It is a gift the likes of which you cannot comprehend. This is your reward," he said, voice laced with a primal snarl that left no room for petty argument. "This is what it is to join the feral court."

"It's true," Sinadim said, his cultured drawl a perfect companion to Giaus' ferocity. "I swear it. But it is a truth you can plainly see standing before you. We are not corrupt. We are *more*."

"Join me," Giaus said. "Bow your heads and submit to my rule. Bend the neck and accept the gifts only I can give you."

"Submit to infection?" one of the twins asked, aghast.

Stomping through the carnage, Giaus flashed a greedy smirk at his audience. His captive subjects. "Each of you will be given the chance to prove yourselves worthy. To survive the killing fever and emerge as something more."

"And if we refuse?" the other twin asked as if the answer wasn't painfully obvious.

"Oblivion." The king's lips spread over a terrible grin. "There is no place for weakness in my Kingdom. Submit or die."

But his moment was overshadowed. Eclipsed by two words spoken in a deep, rumbling voice echoing down from the mouth of the den.

"She's awake."

10

Deep in the dark, at the bottom of a tomb where pitiful little light filtered down from the gloom above, a bleary-eyed blink was the only hint of something profound.

Change, hanging in air too dense to move. A moment with seemingly little significance, and yet... it marked the start of a new era. One that would echo through the ages, surviving change after change, through horrors and triumphs of the unfathomably distant future. A single split second that history would inevitably forget if ever it was recorded at all.

Down in the dark, a nameless harem Omega took her last crackling breath.

In her place, a fledgling queen.

Stretching her lungs and her back, Renegade coughed and rid herself of all that remained of her fever.

War raged in her chest.

A tug that pulled too hard at a thing not meant to unravel. The edges of a blow that struck just a touch too deep.

She could feel them both—her head and chest a mess of tangled things that were and were not. Fears and triumphs, injuries and advantages, her limbs were flush with a strength only half as impressive as the incomparable confidence burning in her heart. A particular poise of spirit that wasn't earned— at least not as a lowly Omega in a prince's harem.

But it was *nothing* to the risen tide pounding at the backside of her ribs. Lust for bloodshed. For sex. A deafening static that left her head spinning as it whirled and slashed, aching one second only to recede in the next. It was static she couldn't ignore, the sort that threatened to consume everything she was or might one day become.

All of it stemming from a bristling cord wound tight about her throat and her heart, tugging in two directions with equal, yet utterly different forces.

A shadow fell across her knees, making her limbs lurch in an uncoordinated flail as she scrambled to flee.

"Renegade?"

Spoken in a voice she recognized. One that forced a memory of kindness. Of big brown eyes set in a shadowed face—a male who'd been kind when he could have been cruel.

"M-Micha?" she rasped, but it was little more than a whisper. Too quiet to make him stay or help or let her beg for freedom from this internment.

He was gone before she could try again. Gone before she could think of a way to plead her case, before she could bargain or beg.

Tongue darting out, Renegade tried to wet dry lips and found herself too parched to succeed. Her mouth gummy from a sleep that had lasted too long.

Pressing her knuckles into her breastbone, she scrubbed at a sense of victory so jubilant, it hurt. Confused by what she felt, for it wasn't her emotion surging through her.

It was *his*.

Theirs.

She felt the earth rumble before she heard it, and even then, it was secondary to the distracting clatter of falling pebbles as they were shaken free from loose shale at the rim of the pit.

Renegade glanced up, unsettled by the trembling beneath her bottom that was echoed in that writhing, barbed noose growing tighter about her soul.

They were footsteps.

Those of a giant trapped in a thundercloud. Sprinting ever closer in the heart of an earthquake, each heavy thud reverberated in her heart and her bones.

Disoriented, she staggered to her feet with all the grace of a newborn kit. Clinging to walls that crumbled beneath her fingertips, she tried to find her balance too late.

A second shadow eclipsed the light and did not linger at the rim of her prison.

He jumped.

Landing with a jarring impact that sent Renegade back to her knees, a mountain crouched before her. Poised on the edge of violence, reeking of sweat. Of blood and danger and potent male pheromones.

It was a scent that staggered. Left her reeling, even as she tried to react, to defend herself from something so obviously dangerous. A scent both colorful and wild, one that left her blinking with wide, mesmerized eyes as looked upon the male who knelt so easily before her.

Giaus.

But not as she remembered him.

This was a beast even the Nine had reason to fear. A conquering radical, every inch the king he claimed to be. Hair and mane matted in blood, in gore and bits of unspeakable horror, Giaus was still. Proud. Letting her look her fill, so she might see what it was she'd bound herself to. Letting her inspect her mate through a new lens.

The Trax. It had bent her perception and let her truly see.

She'd been thrown into the darkness of a prison pit—and upon waking, found herself cloaked in shadows that shivered and shared their secrets. Instead of gloom, Giaus was painted in stark relief. Colors once muted, were now incredibly deep. Displaying a depth she'd never thought to wonder at.

Held in a stiff, proud arc, Giaus' tail flicked just out of sight, the only hint of agitated restraint in a male so ridiculously capable of taking what he wanted. And yet, he remained still for her perusal. Shoulders hunched as if in a bid to appear smaller, less threatening to the fledgling queen trapped in the dark.

Utterly at his mercy.

So she looked. Seeing him with new eyes, and extreme detail.

Enslaved to her own nature, she grew slick with want. Lured by the drive to be the balm to his aches and pains.

The prize for his conquest.

The Omega to his Alpha.

"*No.*"

It was a word forced through clenched teeth. A denial and a challenge for the king who wished to claim a wildling queen—for her to stand at his side *willingly.*

She could feel it, just there. Giaus' mark, seething in her heart, his every wild emotion flicking through her chest too fast to feel anything but the chaos of his excitement. Alien and wild, he was thrilled by her defiance. Aroused and enraged, his blood searing hot with need. Seeking an outlet in which to slake his bottomless lust.

A chalice he would overfill, just so he could prove his virility.

All of it an invasion she hadn't meant to invite, but couldn't refuse.

Not now, with two tiny poisoned darts lodged behind her ribs. Both making demands of her body. Of her mind and spirit. Feasting at will—giving nothing back.

Renegade's ears flicked back, pressed flat to her skull, even as she drank him in. As she pulled first one, then a second foot beneath her. Refusing the urge to submit, she sent a low hiss spattering between blunted teeth.

Giaus grinned, and it was horrible. Deadly beauty, dipped in the blood of vanquished enemies.

He lunged without warning.

Tossing her bodily over his shoulder, he crouched at the bottom of the pit and exploded. Launching them up and out.

Up. Into the dimly lit den where she'd first claimed a pack.

Out into the sunlight overlooking the barren slope of red rock where she'd trapped them all in a sticky net.

She recoiled with a reedy croak, eyes scorched by the sunlight. Blinded by the glare in a way that washed everything out and left her blinking back wretched tears. Pain lanced straight through her eye sockets and popped out the back of her skull, leaving her with a splintering migraine and haloed auras shimmering around everything the light touched.

What little she could see through lashes all but glued together by sparkling tears, revealed a horror. A place left utterly transformed by the havoc of battle.

Bodies scattered in every direction. Corpses of the damned broken and split asunder, their pieces littered every square foot of red stone made darker where a horde had wandered through their midst, and gone no further.

Gaping at the damage, Renegade retched at the scent of putrid decay, grateful that she was almost blind in the sun. Horrified by the notion of touching one of the infected as Giaus trudged right through the slop.

Oblivious to all of it, he carried her over the hump of a broad shoulder. Her ribs slipping where his skin was wet with gore, pulling where it stuck to grime that had already begun to dry. Bare thighs trapped in an unbreakable band where his fingers were tight enough to dimple, she kicked and flailed and accomplished nothing—succeeding only in exposing the scent of her nudity to air still ripe with the chaos of war.

And then she knew. What had happened here. Who had wrought such devastation with a smile on his face and a song in his heart.

She knew because it was the same alien tune rattling her bones from within. The same gruesome melody that had woken her from a killing fever.

Giaus.

Her mate.

"Put me down!" she snarled, clawing at his back with flimsy nails not meant for defense.

To her shock, the king obeyed. Stooping so he might set her dainty feet against slick stone, offering support until she had her balance once more. An unmovable buttress as she tried to find stable footing in ankle-deep gore, almost completely without depth perception.

Renegade whirled, blunted teeth snapping shut inches from his filthy skin, and the barbs in her heart surged with a sickening pulse of renewed interest.

But still, he did not act. Merely tracked her with the easy slide of that golden, feral glare.

Waiting.

For her to submit. To run, just so he might chase.

Blunted teeth exposed in a dainty snarl, her lower back flexed in an irate twitch of useless muscles a split second before she fell to her haunches. Clinging to the shadows thrown by the looming forest, she ducked. Blinked half a dozen times, pressing the knuckles of her right hand into a puddle of tacky red that held an unsettling depth, she mirrored the male who wore her mark and ignored the intrinsic fear that warned of touching infected blood.

Laughter rang out, merriment in a place of dread. A song that pulled one of her ribs out of place as she was made to twist and see the male whose voice held such dry amusement. "She rejects you, oh mighty king of the beyond."

Sinadim.

The prince—Hadim's exiled son—was covered in a thick layer of grime and sweat. Watching her as he moved to stand a half pace behind Giaus, a gleam of feral gold laced through the brilliant green of his good eye.

And just there, high on his shoulder... her mark.

Her pulse skipped at the sight, a ricochet felt in the cord binding them as the fog evaporated from her memory. A bond that had all but split her asunder. One half for Giaus, the other for Sinadim.

Precious little left for her.

A low rumble brought her attention back to the king. Teasing her ears and her fluttering heart all at once, she took a step toward that delicious sound. Enticed as she watched him posture. Watched his mane flare hot and possessive, broadcasting his scent as he met her with an unblinking glare.

And it was then, as she braced for a battle, that she took note of the loose ring of bodies surrounding her.

Males of the pack, picking their way through the killing field to watch.

Micha, Keever and Konjo. The hybrids were clean in a way her Anhur were not. Spared this battle between the infected, their eyes absent any trace of the virus.

Twisting her neck, she looked and saw no hint of the war chief and felt no urge to search among the heaps of dead. But the same could not be said of the smallest male. Her counterpart, the one she'd chosen first.

"Sickle?" she asked, gaze darting from face to face.

Giaus snarled, seething that he was being made to address another male, but he said, "The Unworthy spoke of him in the heat of battle."

"Balkazar mentioned Sickle?" Sinadim barked, tearing his eyes away from Renegade's nudity to demand clarification.

With an irate flick of his tail, Giaus nodded.

But despite Sinadim's curse, they all knew what that meant. What fate held for the little male who couldn't possibly fight a horde without a pack.

"Gone," she murmured, and she hated the way the word felt in her mouth. Sour. Wrong.

And if the wetness on her cheeks was more than just the pain of light-sensitive eyes, she blinked it all away. Letting the light sear her retinas so they couldn't guess at her weakness, her attention flicked back to the mountain standing a full head above the rest.

Quick calculations raced through her

mind as she tried to catch up. Oblivious to her nudity, she crouched in the center of a loose semicircle of raging testosterone. Ears flicking back and forth.

In the end, it was Giaus who claimed her attention. The very sight of him standing there caked in filth, posturing for her perusal, made her throat itch. Aching to unleash that sweet Omega purr that might soothe the king of the wilds and tame him for her pleasure.

"You seek the spoils of victory," she said at length and pulled her feet more firmly beneath her. "A reward for the violence you've dealt today."

It wasn't a question.

"A gift," he rumbled, mane bristling about his shoulders as he sent a surge of Anhur hunger dancing through her blood. "For my Omega."

Renegade's lips twitched, and she did not blink. "I'm not your Omega," she drawled, coy because she knew just how much he wanted to see her temper flare. Just how much denying him would rankle and arouse. Perched on all fours, her hands braced in the muck between the balls of her feet, she let her knees fall apart and set a trap made to torment the male eye. Knew exactly how these males would see the bulge of her breasts when they were pressed together, and she knew just how it would entice when they were given a hint of what lay between her thighs. "I'm not a womb for you to fill with soldiers."

Something vicious gleamed in feral eyes. First from Giaus, who openly adjusted the length of a swollen prick, and then from Sinadim, who did it discreetly as the link between them grew sick with both rejection and helpless attraction all at once.

"You've come seeking a war bride," she continued, rising to stand in his shadow as she addressed Giaus and made a show of it for Sinadim.

Thunder rolled through Giaus' chest but he didn't move. Not a muscle so much as twitched as she picked her way through, closing the distance between them with careful steps.

"You've laid a hundred corpses at my feet," she said and took a step that landed on a body still warm with what had once passed for life out in the beyond. "Fought a battle that surely sent terror into the hearts of the Nine themselves, with only your general at your side."

Sinadim's mane flared, and though he dared not step between them, he couldn't help but posture. Arousal pulsed through him into her. Lust that was chased by a stiff shot of loathing and rejection fueled by the thrill of something taboo he shouldn't want.

Potent enough that she glanced his way, just for a moment. Just to make it hurt before her attention returned to Giaus.

Hips rolling, feet placed to highlight the modest curves she possessed, Renegade's lips twitched at the edges. "Wholesale slaughter just to show your worth. That you deserve the mark I put on your shoulder."

She reached, dainty fingers closing the distance between them as she traced the spot already healed, high atop Giaus' shoulder.

A silver ring of scars that bound her to the beast—almost obliterated by a fresh wound from a mutated jaw.

"And yet..." She trilled, high and elegant at the back of her throat, circling a broad, blood-soaked back. Fingertips trailing through the muck, she painted little swirls as she scraped away at the surface and revealed the tint of bronzed skin lurking beneath. She turned away with a shrug. "And yet, you're no better than the worst of them."

Giaus flinched, head snapping down to scowl at her in open disbelief.

"You come seeking a war bride," she said again. "You drop trinkets at my feet and expect me to lift the tail in awe at your mighty prowess." A low hiss spattered over her lips as her ears flicked back. As her feet slid apart and she assumed a battle position. "You offer insult in place of tribute."

"And what," Giaus asked, feral amusement gleaming in amber eyes, "does my vicious mate require of her king?"

"I am not your womb. Not a mewling cunt to stuff full of soldiers, doomed to die in your petty Anhur wars." She circled, crouched low. Oblivious to the horror squishing between her digits. "I said you would be a king," she murmured, low enough that they were made to strain for the honor of her words. Her first decree. "I gave you a general with royal blood. My gift," she said through a sneer, without bothering to so much as glance in Sinadim's direction. "But a king without a queen is nothing at all, and my submission is not free."

She paused to hold their attention. Letting the silence reign, to give this moment —*her moment*—the weight it was due.

And then, because Giaus had already done it, she said, "You will kneel," through a devious smile. "Kneel and pay proper tribute to your queen."

The poisoned darts in her chest shivered with a violent yawn. One that threatened to tear her ribs from her spine as her heart was split right down the middle.

Conflict.

From Giaus, a vicious hunger. Desire that tore through her blood and ached to see her bend to his rule—even if it cost him a sullied, bent knee. From Sinadim, savage rejection. Hatred of all that she was, all that she'd become. To him, to the fledgling kingdom rising in the wilds, but most of all... sick, twisted loathing of himself for needing his mate to want him, too.

She smiled.

And it was dreadful.

11

For a moment, as he towered above her, Giaus considered the cunning warrior before him. The echo of her demands left chattering on the wind as he stared deep into her eyes. As he took in every aspect of the female who'd done what he feared impossible—and survived the killing fever.

And by the Nine in their firey halls, what a sight stood before him now!

Crouched low in the aftermath of the horde, she returned his glare. Matching his temper, beat for beat. Reeking of belonging. Of ownership. Bold, as an Omega had no right to be. Her ears laid out, tucked tight to her skull in a display of temper—not fear— his precious mate readied herself for battle. Against *him*. Preparing to rail and resist, to claim her place not at his feet, where he'd prepared to host her in pampered comfort, but by his side.

A true queen.

But it was her eyes that had his mane standing on end, his cock stiff and bloated where it hung heavy between his thighs. On proud display.

Pupils blown wide, her irises were a tight ring of gleaming feral gold. Alien. Striking.

Gorgeous.

Giaus had never used the word before Renegade. There had never been a need.

And so, before a pack of males he'd taken by force, he did as the tiny, budding queen demanded.

He knelt.

Because it cost him nothing to do so.

Because he had nothing left to prove.

Because here, among lesser males, a heap of dead, and all the wild, untamed madness thriving in this feral court, Giaus was king. Uncontested. Dominant. Ruthlessly superior, he'd proven himself worthy of the tiny creature demanding his loyalty, for even then, with his knees soaked in blood, Giaus towered above her. Dressing her in shadows that suited her so well.

But the reward of bending for her? It sent blood rushing to his cock in a giddy surge of violent need.

Renegade's lips parted on a shocked breath as the fight abandoned her. Replaced by everything he felt for her, the need to lift the tail for her mate replaced all that conflict. As she softened before him, her ears flicking forward and back. Wide, luminous eyes blinking once, twice before her tongue darted out. Too new to send that taste over the roof of her mouth, to taste his need on the wind the way he'd already tasted hers.

Teaching her would be a joy.

"Come," he drawled, and extended his hand, fingers absent the deadly point of hooked claws he'd happily spent in her defense. Still grimy with murder. "Take what you have earned, my precious mate." He flashed a quick, deadly smile. "My Renegade queen."

Still, she remained. Seemingly torn between want and stubborn defiance.

"Ah," he breathed, breath laced with the faintest edges of a drugging, noxious purr. "Shall I send them all to their knees for you?" he asked, humming low at the back of his throat. Withdrawing his touch, he turned it back upon himself. Fingers spread across his chest, his palm trickling down, over the ridges of muscle and scars. Over his belly button and into the thatch of dark hair trailing down, his fingers traced a path her gaze couldn't help but follow. "Will that soothe your vicious heart, sweet Renegade? Or do you need something"—he took his prick in hand, pumping in a slow pass that drew up a bead of pearly want—"*more*. Something to match that sweet temper?"

She shook her head.

Lashes thick with puzzling wetness, her

pupils were luminous, even in the glare of the sun. Dark and ringed in gleaming, feral gold, she glanced at his face as if helpless to deny herself. Still nervous to be in his presence, still trying to deny the comfort he offered, though she no longer bothered to conceal her nudity.

Instead, her lips parted on a silent gasp, and he knew she could feel it. His need for her. It was there in the way her thighs pressed together. The way slick dropped from a drooling slit, golden ambrosia enticing her mate to fall into the rut. To be enslaved to her, exactly the way Sinadim had warned him against.

"Then come," he said again and grinned when she watched that slow pass of his fist. Pumping up... then down. "Take your reward. Yield to me as I have done for you. Let me tame the fire that pleases me so. Here. Now," he murmured, sure to use every drop of leverage he possessed. Flooding her inferior system with a rush of the demand pounding through his veins. "Be mine before the eyes of these males I have claimed in your name. A queen, truly. But not in the way of the corrupt fools in the Silver City, to whom the title is merely another word for 'breeding wife'. You, sweet ferocious Renegade, shall be a queen in the ways of the ancients. Mounted, knotted, and bred before the pack—*absolutely*, yes. There can be no question whose seed fills you. But here, you will rule at my side. Second only to my wishes."

Using her Hathorian curse, the mating bond, against her, Giaus grinned. Knowing he'd already won. That there wasn't a need to cajole or flirt, but to claim her, here, in this way... it was his pleasure to use her every weakness to his advantage and feel no remorse for doing so. Just as it was his joy to lavish her with her every insatiable want, to pamper and spoil the female who'd claimed him.

In an instant, her ears flicked back. Pupils narrowed to seething pricks of rebellion. Fists clenched at her sides, she showed the smooth line of her teeth, and said, "I will not be a sleeve for your cock! You will yield to *me*. Swear fealty to *me*. Only then will I give you what you so desperately desire. That is my price."

His grin came quick and deadly. Echoed by the distant sound of a trap snapping closed. "Done," he said, only because it was everything he'd ever wanted. And, moving without warning, never leaving his knees, he surged into her. Muscles working in a smooth, effortless arc, he caught her with one hand on her lower back. The other cradling her head.

Delicate where it was needed.

Brutal where it wasn't.

Dumped on her back, Renegade was flipped before her skin touched the gore. Positioned on all fours, a feast spread before him. Her thighs widened to accommodate, not a second was wasted on the courting of a female already dripping for him. Ready to be bred and submitted. Knotted placid as his seed took root.

No, this was a victory lap.

A conquering. Of his mate. Of the wilds. And of this ragged pack of males who would create the foundation of his kingdom. All of them claimed.

For her.

Mane standing on end, Giaus took himself in hand and sent his knob through all that delectable Hathorian cream. Wetting his helm, his tail held high—arrogant and stiff—he sent the fingers of his free hand to tangle in the glossy black silk he loved so dearly, and wrenched her head back. Keeping her from sagging into the muck, even as he prepared to mount her in the middle of an ocean of carnage. Before an audience of males who could look but never touch again.

"You are mine," he snarled, lips hovering scant inches from the shell of delicate ears. Words spoken not just for her benefit, his wicked glare slid up... and found Sinadim at the ready. The other male all but vibrating with the need Giaus alone would slake.

Offering only a smirk, Giaus pressed forward. Slow. With a single leisurely stroke, he bullied his way inside and didn't so much as blink as he did it. Showing Sinadim just where he belonged in their twisted trio.

Renegade shuddered beneath him. Lower back bunched where her tail would have flicked up and away, lifted for him. The way cleared of any obstruction. Her breaths came short and shallow as she tried to accommodate a girth meant for an altogether different species, Renegade arched as she mewled.

"Sing for me," the king murmured, and felt his knot bloom early. Desperate to lock inside her and fuck a litter of hybrids so deep inside she'd be pregnant for the rest of her life. Fat and swollen with him. Only him.

Hands slapping at blood-soaked stone, Renegade took a breath—and exhaled a delectable purr. Serenading them with the notes of a throbbing, delicate melody that bubbled up from the deep past, it was an ethereal coo that hooked him behind the nose and led him to ruin.

He couldn't help but groan at even the barest whisper of that sound.

It was a drug that held them all in thrall. Hybrid and Anhur alike. A beautiful song he tried not to judder as he withdrew, hypnotized by the sight of all that stretched and bloodless sodden flesh. As he spread the globes of her ass with a hand more than twice the size of one full cheek, just so he might admire that tight pucker dimpled and winking by his invasion. His heart hurting for the scar where her tail had been.

Pacing just outside of his reach, Sinadim's mane bristled. Denied access to touch the female who'd marked him. The gleam of newly feral eyes never left the place where king and queen were joined.

"Sing for your mate," Giaus said, taunting as he pressed all the deeper. Returning her song, his chest vibrated with the mangled thing he called a purr. Filling her with a nearly sub-audible rattle that turned her bones to jelly. Until she was held aloft by his hands, thick cock, and little else.

Sinadim snarled, besieged with a deadly rush that had no outlet. None he dared act on —even with the advantage of the rut coursing through his veins—for to do so was to invite a confrontation he could not win.

One he'd already lost, and lost badly.

Grinning, leaning into the cruelty, Giaus shunted forward and filled his queen with everything he had. Stretching all that was wet and wanting, he found her end. Emptied her lungs with an inelegant squawk as their hips clapped together and he bent against that final, hallowed gate he meant to corrupt.

"Good girl," he drawled—and pulled back just to do it again. Deeper this time, ensuring she was made to move around him.

She grunted. Hands scrambling for purchase with every jarring impact of an increasingly frantic pace.

And then she seemed to melt. Accepting his rule, she gave up the fight. Going fluid beneath him, she moved in a sinuous arc of intentional feminine beauty. Flexing that tight sheath in such a way only a Hathorian female could, she fluttered and clenched those fine muscles. Working for it, she fucked him from below. Robbed him of sense with a coy glance over her shoulder, ears tipped forward and back.

"Gorgeous," he breathed, the word torn from the bottom of his lungs, given spontaneous life that redoubled the depths of her purr. Rewarded for the slightest hint of kindness, he shuddered as he rode her, stroking one possessive hand down the length of her spine. Painting pale skin with the stains of her past, Giaus petted where she was marked with ink. A lineage he couldn't read, left by a crueler master than he'd ever be, it was her given name.

The sum total of her value as a harem slave.

It was horror in an elegant scrawl.

A past he'd promised to strike from her skin if she rose up, became the equal of the name she'd chosen... and lived.

Instead, just to defy him, she *thrived.*

Milking him for all he was worth, she took every thick inch. Shunting back for more, she threatened to force his knot well before he'd finished with her.

And though it was in him to let her, to be selfish and take his pleasure from willing, nubile flesh, there was more at play here than simply breeding this wildling girl before an audience.

A statement to be made.

A rival to be subdued.

Nape growing tight, Giaus' glare snapped back to Sinadim. Watching the other male swallow and swallow again. Tasting that forbidden fruit in the way only one of Giaus' line could do, Sinadim cherished every claimed inch of her.

Giaus could see it. Plainly. In the way Sinadim's good eye reflected the light, his working pupil a wide, black disk. In each daring millimeter claimed as the general circled ever closer to the rutting pair.

"Take it," Sinadim whispered, entranced as he watched. Peppering the air with the scent of desperate denial, and he too fell to his knees before the queen. Paying tribute, though he dared not touch. "Take it all, Renegade." Swallowing, he painted her scent along the roof of his mouth and claimed what little slick he could from the air. "Show me what a queen can do for her king. That you were meant for this."

She shivered, neck twisting at the sound of those dulcet tones until she found the face marked by scars. The half-blind prince.

Her second mate.

"That's it," Sinadim breathed and fished his prick from ragged pants. An almost mindless action. "Be a good girl for him, you filthy little whore."

A warning rumble filled Giaus' chest, but Sinadim paid him no mind. Seemed that he couldn't, taken as he was by the rut.

"P-Please," Renegade gasped, choking on a sob. Her attention locked on the other male. Her cheeks growing red as her eyes glassed over with a fog of lust, rimmed in an intense, brilliant ring of gold. "I—I need... more."

Shuffling closer, Sinadim's fist went to his root and squeezed with crushing force. Until the tip of his prick purpled, his knot denied. A pearly drop of seed gushed at his slit. Swiped away by the pad of his free thumb...

... only to be offered to slackened lips and a greedy tongue.

She lunged for that sticky digit. Pulling it between her teeth before Giaus could react. Before he might snatch Sinadim's wrist away and leave it dangling from a new elbow.

Renegade ignited.

Going wild beneath him, Giaus was rewarded for Sinadim's daring. Reaping the benefit, he went still just so he might feel the clenching waves of her orgasm as it rippled along his shaft. The bulging glands nestled deep inside her as she tried to entice him to spill all that frothed and virile seed.

"That's it," Sinadim cooed, panting as he watched. On his knees before the breeding pair, he inserted himself in their moment. Bold, in the manner of one born to privilege. "Again. Show him just what you were trained to do. Take all of him."

Cruel words spoken without heat. An echo Giaus couldn't place, despite the way his mane bristled as a primal snarl burst from his lungs. Tail flagging, the king's sack grew tight, his grip leaving delicious bruises on Renegade's curves. Greedy little marks meant to catch Sinadim's good eye—to twist that jealous blade just a little deeper...

"Show him," Sinadim urged, forcing a snarl to spatter through his teeth, harsh as he glared down the length of an aristocratic nose and hooded lashes. Exquisite pain etched across his brow as he strangled his dick and pelted her with lewd commands. "Show him what an Omega can *really* do for royalty."

Quaking, she took all Giaus had. That tight sheath growing warm in a way that had the new king's hips snapping helplessly forward in shocked delight. Selfish, he was made to obey. His knot forced to bloom by an unnatural, searing heat shimmering deep inside her core.

And with a final, vicious thrust, he was seated deep as he could possibly reach. Bending against her limit, his fingers kneading at tender muscle, he spread her lips and made room. Knot locking into place behind the hooked bone of her pelvis—only to be throttled by a vice of intimate muscle that held him still. Forcing him to stay as his sack rose up, balls spreading to either side of that thick shaft. His seed spilled in a violent flood that dragged pulse after pulse from his very core. Left him coming hard enough that he shook with every jet of semen spilled on a curse.

As if possessed by the Nine, Renegade lunged.

Claiming Sinadim in a single greedy gulp, she took him all the way down—choked on it—and swallowed what she was due.

Roaring, Sinadim's fist cradled her jaw. Her throat and cheek. Fingers trembling as he too emptied himself at the queen's demand.

Still shuddering into the precious creature, Giaus filled her womb with enough seed to make her bulge with it. With him. Pumping her overfull, his vision went black at the edges. Sparkling with the lack of oxygen, for he'd been taken by a divine force. His every muscle locked as his tail flicked in time with the crashing waves kicking sperm through the gates of that hallowed womb.

Ancient primal instinct mutated by the virus, their bond had become something new. Something so utterly enthralling, Giaus' breath was torn from his lungs just as his essence was dragged from his balls.

And then she began to purr.

Singing to her males.

Contented, she uttered that sweet song of a well-bred Omega. Sending the melody through her nose as gulped down the last dregs of royal brine, only to pull back with a lewd, sucking *pop!* and left Sinadim throbbing on his knees as she lapped at any hint of overlooked cream.

Drinking deeply, working the bulge of an impossibly thick knot, she was the bridge between them. The link bonding the males of the feral court.

And for a moment, as Giaus met held Sinadim's mismatched gaze, he again considered how easy it might be to reach out and throttle his rival.

But the moment was fleeting...

... soothed by his queen and the divine heat milking him dry.

12

Drawing a shuddering breath through his teeth, Sinadim staggered to his feet, a string of sperm and drool linking him to swollen lips. A long, glittering tether that sagged before it snapped. Before Giaus wrapped both hands around her middle, fingers almost touching when he stood and took Renegade with him.

Still speared on that massive, captured knot, her cunt was stretched and bloodless. Put on lewd display for any who might look, she was spread before the pack. Delicate petals peeled apart by big hands, Giaus' fingers fanned out as he widened her thighs and showed them all.

That she hadn't spilled a single drop of what he'd pumped so deep inside.

Rippling around a column of captured flesh, she tipped her chin back, unashamed. The back of her head settled in a hollow notch on the king's shoulder, right where her mark sat, her throat exposed as she was ferried away from the carnage Giaus' had dealt.

Something ugly writhed in Sinadim's chest at the sight.

A jaundiced, irrational thing that defied any hint of logic even as it sent his tongue to paint the roof of his mouth. Coating the sensory pits, he fell into the kaleidoscope of divine Sight, just so he might tease her scent free of the others and follow where only Giaus had gone before.

Slick.

Shimmering. Golden. A lure of readiness and temptation—wrapped in the threat of death. The stench of a thing already owned by another, greater male.

It made his sack swell with desperate want. With the need to compete. To purr and soothe and court this devious female who dared taint his hallowed bloodline, if only so he might see her humbled before him. Begging for his knot as she gushed all that glorious, Hathorian cream.

Blackened eyes fluttered open. At first, showing nothing but the whites as pleasure continued to crash against her feeble Hathorian mind... and then, on a tiny, delicate frown, she focused. Sharpened. Rings of feral gold catching the light as she looked.

But it was not the face of her king she sought.

Without a hint of hesitation, without confusion or desperate searching, her gaze landed on *him*. Unerringly.

Because they were linked.

Because she felt what he'd never admit was real.

Because she *knew*.

And in that moment... he hated her for it.

Deeply.

Renegade blinked, just the once before she glanced down. Eyes landing on the still throbbing prick that shone with her spittle. Still oozing seed for the Omega in desperate need of breeding. Of humility or a lesson in respect, he wasn't sure.

Greedy and cruel all at once, she grinned down the length of her nose. And, as if reminding him who was *really* the slave here, a pleased coo spilled over her lips. Mocking his addiction as her hands traced over the jagged edge of her hips, framing Giaus' fingers where he held her in a possessive grip before she moved up. To cup the full curve of ripe tits. Rolling tight, beaded little nipples between her forefingers and thumbs.

His balls flexed. Belching up another rush of unwanted seed as he watched, his throat too dry voice the desperate thirst clawing at his nape.

With a sinuous twist of feminine strength and flexibility, she stretched in Giaus' arms. Her gaze reserved for Sinadim as she showed off all that shining, pale skin and worked to milk another. The erotic show was his never-ending torment, his punishment and anguish as she danced and let the shadows play over each bump of her ribs. Those perfect grooves where his fingers ached to slot.

A throbbing growl rumbled over Sinadim's teeth. His mane flaring in a brief, irritated halo about his shoulders.

She countered with rolling hips and a display of stretched, pale flesh. Teasing him with a glimpse of what he hated himself for wanting...

... and couldn't possibly go without.

But he knew more about her kind than she knew about herself. And almost without meaning to, Sinadim's hand slipped down. Taking himself in hand, he palmed the frantic pulse making his cock ache, and stroked it from root to shining tip.

Using their one-way bond as the weapon it was.

Back arching, she moaned, and her pupils yawned wide as they might go. Leaving nothing but a tight ring of feral gold at their rim, she graced him with a lazy smirk and bade him follow with a jerk of her chin. The idle flick of one ear an invitation he obeyed without pause.

Careless. Drunk on arrogance and orgasms, Renegade licked the smirk that flicked across her lips and did not blink. From right to left, the tip of that pink tongue sent obscene images tumbling through Sinadim's mind as he watched. Helpless. Cock lurching in her direction, he stumbled after the pair despite the angst.

Just a half-step behind.

Not quite lurking in Giaus' shadow.

Too smart to take the lead.

Unable to turn away from the beguiling queen.

The giant ignored him. Utterly taken by so tiny a creature, Giaus cradled his female in arms meant for destruction and walked through the gathered males. Letting horror squelch between his toes, his tail flicked. A flag no other could raise.

Jealousy bubbled at the back of Sinadim's throat.

Twitching muscles came alive, muscles that itched to work as a fog of pheromones and musk rose from heated skin. And just above the hemline of his tattered, ruined pants, Sinadim's lower back lurched with the ghosts of everything that had been taken from him, as if to compete in a game he'd already lost.

Air vibrated through his sinuses, wind that whispered a haunting melody that grew louder the longer he stared after the renegade Omega. Their tiny, toothless Hathorian mate.

The death queen.

Sinadim's throat trembled with a song he'd never thought to sing for any—let alone a mere harem slave who'd almost certainly murdered him with her cursed bite. It was the sound of embers crackling in a banked fire. Kindling burning up in a ravenous blaze of aching need.

His purr.

Born of envy and self-loathing, it was rebellion and unquenchable lust. A spiteful fire burning in the cauldron caged behind his ribs, for he was made to watch as Renegade pressed a kiss to the underside of Giaus' jaw. A fallen prince made passive observer of dainty fingers tracing stubble and scars, ordered to follow when he'd been born to rule.

And there, just for a moment, something truly wicked flickered in the depths of eyes no longer blank and glossy.

Renegade turned her head in a sinuous curl of bare flesh and cruel intentions...

... and set her attention upon Giaus.

Lavishing adoration on her king, she passed Sinadim over with an ease that burned with more acid than a slap.

Sinadim jerked. Sweat blooming on his forehead with the shock of it. As if struck by an icy wash of painful neglect.

Mane flaring up around his shoulders, Sinadim ground his molars and choked on that rising bubble of kindness and temptation. He killed any whisper of a drugging purr as he stalked Giaus' footsteps, tipped his chin back, and tasted the golden trail of slick shimmering on the breeze.

Seething.

Hurt.

Giaus glanced back and down, pinning Sinadim with a molten glare that promised gruesome punishment should he dare to insert himself between them. It was there in his posture, in the brief lurching twitch of his dense mane and the irate flick of his tail.

Claws curled into the heart of his palms, Sinadim took a concentrated breath. Forced himself to watch when the king ascended the natural hewn steps leading to the den. When he turned, stepped bodily into the uppermost pool of heated, swirling water, and sank into the hot spring that stank faintly of sulfur.

Renegade hissed as she was engulfed.

Purred when Giaus settled back and sluiced through the seeded walls of that tight sheath.

Grinning, her eyes fluttered and rolled when the king found the swollen bead of her clit and sent his thumb to trace happy little circles that saw her jaw go slack. Loopy, barely conscious, she let her head fall back, shivering with the sort of supreme satisfaction only a Hathorian female might ever know.

Sedated by Giaus' knot—by his touch and his purr and his every ounce of undivided, feral attention—she forgot to beg for Sinadim. Left the prince trembling with the misery of neglect as she was tended by her mate... for of course... either of them would do...

... and Sinadim didn't quite measure up.

But a smile twitched into being, for he still had one last secret to play.

One that would secure him in place as an eternal irritant to the king he'd sworn to serve.

"I have said we shall build a kingdom," Giaus began, and left her draped across his thighs as he settled back. As the water washed away much of the gore drying on his skin, he spread his arms over the rim of the hot spring and let her work his length at her leisure. The king was content to watch the muscles in her back flex as she rode that massive knot. "I have said I have no interest in the wars of weak males swaddled in luxury," Giaus drawled and sent blunted fingers through the tangles of black silk. Twisting his digits through her hair, he worked to untangle ropes of glossy pitch so they might cascade down the length of her spine. "I meant to let you prove your worth," he added and glanced at those gathered around the hot spring. "To die forgotten, if that was the will of the Nine."

Refusing to submit, Sinadim tore himself free of his ruined clothing and splashed into the hot water. Arrogant, drawn by the ripple of waves lapping at pinkened skin, his mismatched gaze remained fixed to Renegade's slender frame as he sat. Bold when he said, "King of nothing," and thumbed the ridge of scars that no longer wept or itched. "A ruler without a throne or legacy."

"I was wrong," Giaus said, *easily*. Admitting fault with a smirk thrown over the crown of Renegade's hair, acknowledging the barb without bothering to muster any heat. "I've conquered much... survived the wilds long enough to forget the passing seasons. *Alone*. I've seen darkness more terrible than you can possibly imagine, survived nightmares and slaughtered giants with ease. But the nuances of brotherhood"—he shrugged—"eludes me."

Falling in around them, Micha, Keever, and Konjo kept a wary distance. Leery of infection, intrigued by the impossible nature of what they'd seen Giaus do in spite of their blood oath to a pack that was no more.

"Sinadim begged for your lives," Giaus went on. "He saved you when I was content to let you rot."

Micha's sparse mane stood on end, his voice a deep boom of droll sarcasm. "If this is your great speech to convince us to let go of all our convictions, you're leaving much to be desired."

Giaus' grin only grew. A knowing fire blazing in a moment of shared knowledge between them, for with a seductive rattle passing over his lips, Giaus' chin tilted back. To taste the wind, his pupils blooming as he fell into the Sight.

"We saw what became of Balkazar," Micha added, oblivious to the divinity shimmering right in front of them. "The war chief is sick with the very pestilence you offer as a reward for this... madness. Vile and corrupt. No different than the diseased miscreants you just dispatched so effortlessly. What promise can you possibly make to assure us we aren't doomed for that same fate?"

For a moment, there was only the gentle slap of water disturbed by the queen.

And then amber eyes flicked up and found an anchor on Sinadim's face, and he knew. What Giaus wanted of him. Why he'd been permitted to stay and sit so close.

It was the illusion of unity.

"*I* am that promise," Sinadim murmured, unable to keep his eye from wandering back to jiggling breasts topped with rosy nipples dancing just out of reach. His cock grew painfully thick beneath warm water. "Balkazar," he murmured and made fleeting eye contact with the king as he stirred the water with his claws, "is Giaus' creation. Not *hers*."

And then, sending those claws to trace the imprint of blunted teeth, Sinadim showed them what Renegade had done. That Giaus was not the only one claimed by the queen.

"There is a new variant," Sinadim said. "A third. One born of your mother's people. Hathorian, not Anhur."

Sparse mane flaring about broad, dark shoulders, Micha sucked a breath through his teeth. His gaze snapped back to the prize cradled in Giaus' arms. "Impossible," Micha whispered at length, denying it, despite the light of understanding gleaming from within. Unable to tear his eyes from the rosy cheeks of the female spread and stuffed on Giaus' lap. "*Your* queen," he said reluctantly. "*Our* risk. No guarantees that we'll survive the killing fever as you have. Changed. Graced with this incredible strength and speed." Micha's nose wrinkled, and with a boldness Sinadim had never seen from the hybrid warrior, he dared to prod a ring of teeth that had almost obliterated Renegade's coveted mating mark left high on Giaus' shoulder. "Twice infected, yet seemingly immune to the original strain."

"It's true, the virus kills more often than it doesn't," Giaus said, voice a deep rumble of words over gravel as he addressed the hybrids. "True that I have no reason to fear infection from a thing I alone have mastered. And it is true," he growled and moved to grip Renegade's hips as they rolled and worked on his lap, "that there are things out here you cannot imagine. Dangers spawned from the ashes of our ancestors, fed by the fools who throw precious things over the wall." Giaus' mane flared, and he crushed Renegade's back to his front. One massive arm wrapped tight about her middle, he brought her close as her fragile bones could bear. "Fools who discard Hathorians like trash because they're blinded by fear. Content to let you die in pointless wars, they grow fat while we are left mutilated and starving. Our tails docked for daring to want just a taste of what the elite horde.

"There is no promise of a happy ending in the feral court—only the eventuality that you will fall to the Trax, one and all." Giaus shrugged. "I offer the luxury of hope. A chance for more, if you're bold enough to take it, for this is a test of your loyalty," he murmured, and his hands dipped below the surface to seize the cradle of Renegade's hips. Shunting deeper as he guided her to ride, and ride hard. "Not to me. Not to any mere Anhur master who proves himself worthy of your skill. This is a test of loyalty to your queen. This precious female who shall birth a new era, who carries inside her the very blood of the Nine."

At this, Renegade's glare grew sharp. Vicious with defiance. "I will not—"

But before she might react, before she could deny that she'd breed high-quality hybrids for them, Giaus uttered a song meant to enslave and cherish. Lips pressed into her hair, he soothed the girl with a throbbing purr that sent mayhem spiraling through Sinadim's senses and had him swallowing the threads of competition once more.

Her rebellion was enough to send Giaus over the edge. Succumbing to the tug and pull of his mate's cunt, he snarled. Buried himself hard, tail lashing beneath the surface of warm water. Battering at the spot where she held him fast and wouldn't let go, only to feel her come apart on his knob. Where they could all see the clenching grip she had on him.

As if unaffected by so sordid a display, Micha tilted his dark head and frowned. "Build a kingdom in the fashion of the old ways? *Here*?"

"'*Here*' is defensible," Giaus returned. Panting as a drop of sweat trickled through the grime misting his cheeks. "A wall at our backs. Forest and river everywhere else." And then the king paused in his sermon. Hesitating, when he said, "There are packs. Hordes of infected like the one you saw today. Mindless, roaming beasts who serve but a single master."

It was Sinadim who bristled. Sinadim who caught the swirling undertone of worry laced in Giaus' deep voice. "You've seen it," he said. "This beast you won't name."

Giaus stilled. "It is a darkness that swallows everything in its path. It owns the hordes. Commands the Legion." At this, a shiver went through the king. Disguised in the bubbling waters—felt beneath the surface by a fallen prince. "The infected are driven to collect fodder for the great roaming armies patrolling these woods. Females for a massive diseased harem. Rare is the male who can resist the call of the Legion, as I have done. For it never stops calling..."

Sinadim's jaw flexed, the muscle jumping in agitation.

"I have told you to join me or face oblivion," Giaus said. "That there is no room for weakness in my kingdom. And it's true—guarding my mate will be no easy task. Fortifying this queen's landing will be grueling work. But this is the price of your exile from the Silver City.

Giaus paused then, touching them all with the light of his feral gaze. "Choose. To fall, as Balkazar fell. Infected by a variant that favors oblivion, fall to the command of the legion, enslaved to the many, where you will be made to turn against your brothers. Or chose this tiny, glorious Hathorian queen who offers hope. Hope that in her, the virus has become something divine for Anhur, Hathorian, and hybrid alike."

That might have been the end of it. Might have been enough to win the loyalty of the hybrids who'd once been Sinadim's loyal men. But with a cruel smirk, Sinadim watched the hybrids wander away to consider their options, then said, "It's not enough."

Head tipped back, menace rumbled through Giaus' chest. A promise of retribution that went ignored.

"It's not enough to make them choose and swear loyalty to a defective queen."

At this Giaus went very still, his eyes little more than gleaming slits.

"It's not enough to name a general, and it's not enough to abstain from tasting her slick," Sinadim said and allowed his mismatched gaze to slip to Renegade's nudity once more. "This kingdom of yours will fail."

"Is that so?"

"I have one last secret," Sinadim drawled, claws circling as he watched the king and did not blink. "One last coveted scrap to divulge, and without it, everything you want is doomed to fail."

For a moment, there was silence. The gentle murmur of lapping water and the distant whistle of wind through the trees.

And then, "Your price?"

Sinadim grinned, showing teeth, but said nothing...

... because of course, Giaus already knew.

13

Pressing his back to stone, ears flicking back and forth, Sickle scanned the landscape for any hint of lurking predators. Braced for attack. Counting the beats of his heart as he stared at the smoking corpse laid out before him. The brood mother, or...

... what was left of her.

What had once been a breathing nightmare was now a smoldering wreckage of horrors. Leathery, impenetrable skin left sagging from charred bones, every last scrap of meat the brood mother might have possessed had been consumed from the inside. Hollowed out by her own offspring in a final gesture of reptilian love, her massive vacant eye sockets had been left to stare into nothing for the rest of time. Void of everything but twin, fragile tendrils of rancid smoke curling around empty ocular bones.

But it was her jaws—wide enough that he

could fit his head, neck, and shoulders inside and still have room to turn—that spoke of what had happened here. Left jarringly askew, they'd been unhinged by some awesome force, the joint shattered high at the connecting point where mandible met skull.

There had been a battle here.

A clash between titans of gruesome proportions, their passage marked by the loser of a contest Sickle was glad he hadn't witnessed.

Still... he would do well to respect the victor. Absent or not, for it was a predator greater than even the most feared beast in all the great beyond—the only thing marking its passage was the carnage left smoking in its wake.

It was an instinct exclusive to Hathorian males, his compulsion to cling to shadows. Not something a prized harem Omega could possibly know, for although it was true that his female counterparts were kept safe and cherished in secret subterranean vaults... Sickle had been raised in the courts. Traded and marked at the whims of a predatory species, he knew too well what it meant to suffer the consequences of rash decisions.

All the Omega male could do was guess at what had been capable of doing damage like that to a nesting brood mother.

But he did not charge forward, reckless and flush with the excitement of his foundling idea. He refused the urge to celebrate the boon of some greater monster's table scraps, and instead clung to shadows and searched the barren landscape for any hint that that fearsome predator had yet to move on. Searching for a demon lurking in wait, one clever enough to use a corpse as bait to nab an easy meal.

Heavy with the scent of flesh cooked in sulfur, only the wind dared to offer a vague answer, useless though it might be.

Grimacing, ears tucked flat, Sickle inched from the darkness. Ready to bolt back into the tunnels at a moment's notice, his heart hammered at the backs of his eyeballs. Echoing in his ears where it pounded a rhythm in the very tips of his fingers... all the way down to the twisted nub of his severed tail.

It was madness to stay, to make a stand and claim his place among the wild and brutal. He had no weapons, no legendary Anhur strength or speed. All he had was a lifetime of abuse and neglect fueling his thirst for vengeance. For validation that he was here! That he deserved a place to finally close both eyes and sleep well. In safety.

This was that.

A place to build a life, where he might grow into something formidable, free to live or die at his own whim. Where he might know the sort of happiness Renegade had known, the secret glimmer he'd caught when she'd turned glassy eyes back into the wood.

A tiny, sad smile creasing the edges of her lips.

She'd found peace, living in solitude. He was sure of it.

And it might have been enough.

Ears flicked back, pressed to his skull, Sickle steeled himself for the leap.

What he needed most was a way to defend his den against interlopers. An advantage over the razor-sharp instincts of monsters who would see him perish against impossible odds. He needed a way to not only refuse the call of the primordial reptilian queen who demanded he kneel but to maintain his vow to never do so again.

The obsidian glitter pulled him forward. A relentless lure of necessity, it forced his courage to build with every greedy step closer to that gaping maw of pointed, deadly teeth.

He reached. Fingers inching not toward the pointed tips—that had already bloodied his digits with their serrated edge—but to their root. To the band of brittle charcoal keeping them anchored in bone.

It was nothing to wriggle them loose. A joy to watch what had once been gore-soaked gums crumble away at his lightest touch.

One by one, they popped free. Dropped into a tinkling pile of deadly potential, the brood mother's teeth had been tempered by the fires that burned inside all lava-kin. In life, a noxious, organic magma contained in the gullet, but in death, it spilled over and raged out of control. Obliterating what re-mained. Sinew and muscle, bones and fat. Everything...

... except the teeth.

Whatever impossibly hard mineral they were made of had turned to obsidian glass in death.

A gift from the Nine. Gods and Goddesses whose lore he knew well, who'd never both-ered to notice him when he'd been nothing but a queen's plaything. Deities who must now have some stake in his survival... some reason to offer gifts instead of demanding sacrifice.

Some reason that he had survived, in spite of everything.

Change on the wind, and no room for the old-world relics who couldn't adapt.

Sultana would see him hollowed out by her consorts.

Consumed from the inside at her command...

Sickle had nothing but his wit and a hollow corpse, but from that, he meant to give himself claws.

Sixty-two of them, to be exact.

Serrated from point to base, deadly sharp all the way to the root, the canines were as long as his forearm. Perfect for landing the killing blow, only to retreat so any hapless prey might bleed to death. Now repurposed, he fashioned all four canines into curved blades and tucked them into his belt. Two on his outer thighs, the others hidden at his lower back. The rest he kept for tools.

Fifty-eight wicked, glittering black talons that would give even the best Anhur warrior pause.

Grinning now, Sickle showed the point of his own canines as he worked. Turning his attention to the scaly hide that hadn't dimmed or tarnished under extreme heat, he ignored the slice of nicked fingers, wedged his new knives between the scales, and began to cut. Working wet leather with the skill and speed of one made to sew elaborate gowns for his Anhur queens, he pulled two full sets of custom armor from the carcass before the sun yielded to the triplet moons.

And it was then, as he toiled, that he felt the night calling. Seduction from the shadows, there was beauty in the twilight. Peace in the roar of the night things waking to stretch leathery wings and sharpen claws, for in the formless shrieking he heard what lay hidden, and knew.

They were calling him home.

Armored from fingertips to nape, from skull to heels, a new brand of warrior was born in the wilds. One whose tattoos meant nothing where they couldn't be seen. To whom strength and speed were secondary to cunning wit, and the accuracy of a well-placed slice from a blade.

This was a paradise meant for the vicious,

where the wilds refused to suffer the ignorance of fools.

A place where Sickle of the Silver Court couldn't survive, where only a shade of who he'd been might be free to thrive.

Confident, *ready*, the Omega male dragged the remains of the brood mother back into his den. Fingers hooked beneath the edge of a shattered mandible bone, he felt something pop. Something that oozed where his fingers slipped for purchase.

Gooey slime.

A fetid liquid that reeked enough to send him staggering back, retching at the end of every breath. The scent was laced with something that made his nape tight with the unmistakable shiver of fear.

An instinctive thing linked to his olfactory senses. Primal memory of phantoms in the gloom.

He cursed himself for a fool, turning to scrub his palm against the limestone walls of his den—and succeeded only in spreading that sludge in an arc of reeking denial.

Lava-kin stink glands.

It clung like nothing he'd ever encountered. Coating his palm and knuckles in a film of jelly resistant to vigorous scrubbing that only seemed to spread a greasy film of rendered fat over whatever he touched. Leaving him saturated with the scent of a nesting brood mother.

A beacon screaming danger to any who

might venture close enough, or dare entry to this den.

"Fuck," he whispered because it was a foul boon indeed. One he could test on his captive audience.

Abandoning the carcass at the entrance to his den, he turned heel and darted back the way he'd come. Eyes well-adjusted to the gloom, pupils blown wide as they might go, he nipped through the tunnels. Armor light on his back, breathable as he moved at speed.

Sultana was exactly where he'd left her. Her consorts swirling around the tombstone keeping her interred, trying in desperate futility to unleash her wrath.

At the sight of their mother's skin cut, trimmed, and sewn into something new, the males scattered, issuing startled, horrified yelps. Leaving him free to surge forward, take a steadying breath, and kick the lid off Sultana's prison.

A whip of primal fury streaked past his shin. Blurry, sinuous scales that lashed up and out. Moving in a vicious, jagged slash, Sultana landed coiled atop her grave. Frill rippling about her angular cheeks, forefeet braced, she pinned him with a gleaming alien glare and let her jaws fall apart on a rattling, dual-toned hiss.

Before she could issue the command to kill, he flashed his palm wet with the ichor of her mother's potent musk. Let her forked, flicking tongue catch the scent of the congealed jelly glued to his skin and watched when, in an instant, Sultana's crimson frill snapped shut. Tight to her nape as she uttered a new warble. One of terrified submission that tugged at his heart in a way that gave him pause... for it was a sound he recognized.

One he himself had made countless times, as Anhur claws tore through his flesh...

Throat flexing, the Omega male swallowed a lump that only grew as he choked it down. Blinking back the salty burn of helpless memory, for this was what he needed! This was survival, a test of his metal.

He'd be a fool to reject an easy meal for sentiment.

And then Sultana whimpered.

Tail wrapping tight about her hindquarters, she lifted her left forepaw—and rolled. Showing the pale underbelly where he might sheath his obsidian blades and eat well. A statement made with his first meal the flesh of lava-kin. Tender and young.

"It's the law of this place," the Omega whispered and clutched at the hilt of one of his many obsidian knives. Hesitating long enough that his grip grew slick with anxious sweat.

Sultana trembled.

A foul liquid leaked from a gap in the scales tucked neatly beneath her tail.

As if it were the signal they'd been waiting for, the males began to rattle—and it was the sound of a tide turning. Watching through slitted glares as their unblooded queen was tested and found wanting, their muscles bunched as the scent of rejection grew ripe in the air.

"Shit," he hissed and stepped back. Wary of the gathered neonates, whose eyes were filled with an unmistakable gleam.

Murder.

Where he hesitated, the males surged into action. Homicidal eyes fixed not to him, but to the tiny flailing queen who couldn't stop the serpent from consuming its tail.

Five sets of claws skittered against stone.

They were on her before he could take a single, shocked breath. Moving with one mind, frantic squeals rang out. A storm of chaotic need, of neglect and desperate survival, they turned on their queen. Trying to tear at those impenetrable scales while Sultana thrashed and whipped and tried to evade her former consorts.

It was to be her end.

The conclusion written by the vicious nature of where they'd been born, a place where she could either rule or die. Where shades of grey meant nothing more than another day yielding to a violent night... the pattern repeating over and over and over again.

Until someone with the means broke it.

"No," he whispered because no matter his rebirth—that he was to carve a place for himself in lonely wilds—he couldn't sit and watch a queen die. To do that, was to give up the best part of himself.

And so, as if commanded to act, the Omega male surged forward with a war cry of his own. Jaw clenched, ears flat, he plunged an armored fist into the mass of writhing, scaly bodies. Caught a tiny, wriggling serpent and wrenched her free.

He was answered by a frustrated wail, and all five remaining clutchlings set their wrath upon him.

Ignoring the slicing nip of teeth that found chinks in his armor, he held Sultana aloft and swiped at her brethren. Sending two spinning toward the cave wall, only to watch them twist and reset before their tiny claws had even touched stone.

Above him, Sultana's frill snapped open, delicate, yet rigid enough to move his fingers. The boney length of her tail wrapping tight about his wrist, she anchored herself and took a breath.

He felt it when she trilled. Sound vibrating in a miniature chest, it was a brief warning of what was to come.

Panic sweat bloomed across every inch of his skin, triggered by the mere memory of that tri-toned, warbling cry. Bracing, fist clenched, his arm extended as far from his person as he could manage, the Omega male tried to clasp one palm over his ears—the other ear pressed tight to a bunched shoulder. Teeth clenched in preparation of that wretched, piercing howl.

Silence fell for a single precious instant...

... before the males fell away, screeching. Spines twisting, they rubbed their muzzles into the stone floor and left gouges in stone as they scrambled to do more than shiver in agony.

Bewildered, he looked to his clenched fist and saw Sultana in all her ferocious glory. Frill fully open in a crimson flare, her jaws sagged around an unheard scream. A brutal song turned on those wretched peasants who dared to question her rule.

Her frill was directional.

He laughed, then. Giddy with the realization that *this* had been his test. Sultana—and her consorts—were his prize, for with a single stroke from a palm still tacky with the noxious liquid of the brood mother, Sultana was silenced. The other clutchlings were free to stagger to their feet, dazed, panting in the aftermath of so brutal a weapon being used upon them... but alive.

Enthralled once more.

This time to a new master who would see them rise.

"Come, Sultana," he cooed, petting his queen with the point of one obsidian claw, enticing her frill to tuck neatly under her chin once more. "There's work to be done."

14

Uneven jaws gaping, Balkazar panted through a sagging maw. The *thump-pat* of his footfalls lost amongst the cacophony of a thousand *thousand* marching at his back.

No longer hunted... he was being driven.

To what or *where*, he couldn't begin to guess. Not with the swirling, dancing colors casting illusions he couldn't quite see. What had begun to rot, had instead grown hard. Calcified tumors riddled his brain and body, cementing those gruesome changes in place. All that corruption and decay made permanent. The burden of irregular weight distribution now supported by boney growths that made what had once been his left arm—reaching all the way back and around from his shoulder blade to his fingertips—a cumbersome shield at the head of a battering ram.

He'd been transformed.

Utterly.

Swampy lungs belching up a bubble of phlegm, what was left of Balkazar's mane bristled as he trundled through dense brush. Forcing his way *through,* he no longer bothered himself to lash out at the saplings. Couldn't hear their mockery and was no longer slowed by their trickery, the insidious whispers demanding that he join the Legion.

He was they.

They were he.

Swallowed whole in a single gulp, most of what the war chief once was, had been consumed. Made an asset to the many. He ran for days without thinking of food or drink. Stopped to eat a passing mouthful of festering flesh when the horde stumbled across a titanic dead thing in a swamp. Bloated, legs sticking straight up, knees locked in place as it baked in the heat of the mid-day sun, it had died naturally. Picked over by the carrion eaters until the rumble of the approaching horde had chased away all competition.

Jaws working with mindless abandon, Balkazar sought only to fill his empty belly so he might fuel his hideous growth. Chomping on anything warm that squelched.

Mud.

Bone.

Flesh—living, diseased, or very, *very* dead.

It all went in without a thought until the horde pushed forward.

There was but a single act of love that kept him separate, allowing one shining blue eye to skitter *back* as he plodded onward. Back to where he'd come... where a one-eyed prince had risen from the dark with a burning crown atop his head...

... only to find himself eclipsed in the shadow of another. One who burned with a thousand times his brilliance.

Giaus. A mighty king, crowned in starlight and onyx.

If Balkazar had thought slaughtering a nesting brood mother was an impossible feat, it was nothing, *nothing* in the light of what Giaus had done to the horde.

Black flames swirled in his wake, a crackling halo that flickered all around him. The king had made a mockery of the horde fodder. Obliterating them by the dozens with a wild grin, he protected the brothers Balkazar had meant to die for. Poetry in slaughter, it was art in motion. Grace in the elegant twist of spilled entrails, in severed limbs and pools of clumpy gore.

Throat flexing, Balkazar choked back a jealous growl, for he could still taste it. That something both terrible and wondrous. The bright, alluring musk of a male so far beyond the peak of Anhur beauty that there was simply no other way to describe him.

Divine.

His was a scent Balkazar recognized in his

blood before the thought ever reached his diseased brain.

Sire.

If he had been born of Giaus' lineage—not made—that title might have driven Balkazar to attack. To assert himself as dominant, in the manner of a true Anhur warrior. The son perpetually driven to oust the father, to claim the right of succession and prove that he was worthy of his place at the head of a vicious table. His place in this life and the next earned.

But Balkazar had known, from the moment he'd first laid eyes upon the ethereal brutality Giaus wielded with insulting ease, that he was outmatched.

It was just there, had *always* been there, in Giaus' scent.

He was king, and he would defend that title and everything that went with it—Sinadim, Renegade, and his throne—with the sort of possessive rage that blistered any who dared to venture too close.

Balkazar's warning had not been needed.

Sickle's attempt to end them all, to save his precious little whore from a fate she'd been born for?

A failure hardly worthy of note.

The wave of infected had crashed against red stone—and *Giaus*. Stopped with frightening ease by a male who took joy in defending his claim.

All of it without incident. Without Balkazar's headlong race to warn them of Sickle's betrayal.

Because he was irrelevant.

A relic without purpose.

Obsolete. Expendable.

A worthless sack festering tumors, the very sight of which had made Sinadim recoil.

And worse, he'd been replaced. Exchanged for a titan who didn't need permission to breed a high-quality quim, for it was clear, even from the perspective of an outcast, that Giaus had no intention of sharing.

There was nothing he might offer the male who'd taken his place at Sinadim's side. Nothing his beloved prince needed from him, now. Nothing else he could possibly give.

Except his life.

And so, Balkazar had done what little he could. Turned the horde away from the Queen's Landing and fulfilled his blood oath to the Karahmet dynasty, such as it was.

Mowing down a thatch of saplings, he burst through the trees into the clearing of a foggy, rainy day. Lost in the thunder of the horde, he gave himself up for the many. Let them choke on his grief and forget. Just for a moment.

With the dull, lowing intelligence of an opportunistic hunter, his lopsided head fell back. Jaws gaping wide, he licked at the rain. Trying to slurp up what moisture he could. All thoughts of pack and prince forgotten as he drank just enough to remind himself of the brutal, savaging thirst.

It was then, as his thickening hide was washed of the topmost layer of grime, that blue eyes flicked down.

A cliff overlooking a deep valley. Trees that had been felled by the thousands, it was a barren slope eroding and exposed to the elements.

And for a moment, as he looked and saw movement, Balkazar thought he was witness to a mighty mudslide. One that stretched well over the horizon where it spilled over from the valley.

The horde pushed on.

Jostling and fighting for position, they surged over the edge. Filling a narrow path hidden from the top of the ridge, the horde descended in a rush. Careless of any too light or weak to stay on the path, no attention was spared for any who were thrown over the edge. The only hint of their demise was a dull howl that did not echo before it was silenced.

He blinked.

Peering over the thick edge of the bone that had once been his elbow, he squinted at the valley. Brows unable to bunch where the left side had tripled in size, he scowled as best he could.

Movement.

The valley floor was *alive*.

Writhing, twisting, turning back upon itself.

It was the horde.

The *whole* horde, for the branch Balkazar knew was only a fragment of the true size. Of the multitude. And even from his distance, he could see the mutated and grotesque for what they really were... that there was an order in the chaos, ranking assigned to size. A swirling pattern visible only to one of the infected, one who belonged to the many, as Balkazar now belonged.

Despite the urge to surrender, to rejoin the mass of corrupted Anhur, something held him still. Frozen on the edge. Crouching in shadows, he watched. Trying to make sense of what he saw.

It was not a wasted effort.

In the heart of the twisting mass, something moved.

Something of a size that boggled his delicate mind, for it was simply impossible that such a thing could exist.

But there it sat.

In the heart of the Legion, at the bottom of a great pit worn into stone, a Deity held court. A mammoth that took a swing and in a single swipe erased more infected than even Giaus had slaughtered. Jaws gaping wide, it snatched up any too slow to escape. Cannibalizing the dead and the slow, it feasted upon the army hopeless lost.

Thousands flooded in to fill the void.

Even through the rot, Balkazar understood two simple truths.

This army of infected was not the result of a single dynasty banishing dissenters to the wild—this was *generations* of exiled criminals. This was the result of incomprehensible arrogance bred in the Silver City, that assumed no responsibility for the instability fostered by the elite and their large harems that left countless males with nothing to lose. No prospects for a mate, no hope of a legacy.

No future.

And he knew, without a hint of hesitation or doubt, what would happen next. When such a beast caught wind of a certain perfumed cunt of the finest quality. A treacherous little whore who couldn't help but drip for a monster, who'd betray Sinadim and present that gushing slit for a behemoth more titanic than her precious king.

Couldn't be helped. It was, after all, her nature.

A sound shattered the moment. Altered the direction of falling raindrops for an instant as the wave caught up to itself.

Balkazar was thrown off his feet.

Flailing, right sight trying to scramble for purchase, he worked to right himself as the horde grew excited by the call of their master.

Groaning low at the back of his throat, Balkazar fought to stand. Terror of an unknown quality splintered through what remained of his soggy brain, the sort of fear that dictated what came next.

He did not join his kind.

He could not press on with the horde.

One blue eye looked back, to where he'd come. That thing that kept him separate. Enslaved to the echo of the love he'd had for a one-eyed prince. For the king dressed in swirling, crackling flames of inky pitch. And the tiny helpless queen who bound them together with little more than the irresistible lure that wept between her legs.

Turning without conscious thought, the war chief hefted his bulk away. Back, he lumbered through the dregs of the passing splinter of infected, ignoring those too big to do more than glance off his shielded plow. Going straight *through* the rest.

Never noticing the wetness soaking his front, that he'd lost his bladder at the mere existence of what commanded the Legion.

He was a relic with one last purpose.

Expendable in fulfilling his blood oath, that he might die for his prince. His relevance found not in breeding a queen of worth, or destroying the usurper who'd replaced him, but in a single, final act of devotion.

That he might lay down his worthless life for his prince.

15

Gasping, Renegade came awake on a strangled cry. Mouth stuffed with cotton, her tongue dry and thick as her muscles strained against the weight of a powerful orgasm.

Pleasure.

Bliss laced with bolts of pain that tracked up the inside of her pelvis, before exploding in wave after wave of diabolical, clenching delirium. A frantic wriggling pattern she could see in the pulsing vein located somewhere at the back of her eyeballs. It echoed in each spasm of her fluttering pussy, distorting what she saw with every ticking beat of her heart.

A rough hand found its way into her hair, blunted nails scraping at her scalp as her attention was dragged down. As she was forced to see the male who'd rung such a volcanic orgasm from her body. Chin to chest, he filled her bleary gaze.

Rugged. Masculine.

Giaus.

Her chosen king.

And he was not alone.

Twisting, Renegade looked and found the other. Sinadim, in all his haughty, disfigured Karahmet glory.

He tipped his good eye toward her, hiding the mangled half in shadows that, to her, only enhanced the mutilation. Hiding scars she knew all too well, for she bore the same gruesome marks, her skin left twisted by the very same male. Hadim's everlasting touch traced the inside of her right arm, from pit to wrist.

The shared trauma did little to soften the prince toward her.

As she watched, Sinadim's lips spread over a wolfish grin. Teeth bared. Silver eye lit with a ghostly, metallic sheen... the other a vibrant green laced with feral gold. His fist worked in time to Giaus' hips, and just for a moment—if she squinted—it was as if the prince was the one riding her hard and fast. As if he was the one who climaxed, pressing his knob deep as he might go only to be halted at her end.

Giaus snarled and shattered the illusion. His teeth pinching the cone of her left ear, he tipped her hips forward and filled her to overflowing. Each shuddering thrust adding to the creamy mess bubbling from between lips stretched wide as they could go. He withheld his knot and claimed her from the back.

And then, with the rough edge of bloody knuckles, he guided her chin and made her look. Making sure Sinadim could see the helpless pleasure scrawled across her brow, so the other could see where he belonged in Giaus' kingdom.

That he would never be anything but a guest in Giaus' nest.

She could feel it all. The triumph and the hurt. The devious, ravenous, desperate need.

All of it Anhur.

Precious little left for her.

"That's it," Giaus rumbled. His voice a deep hum that could be felt in her marrow, her blood, through the fragile muscles in her heart, and all the way up to the intangible barbed dart hooked around her throat.

That sacred place meant for a Hathorian mate, forever tainted by the stink of two Anhur.

She felt it when he came, as if that thick, spurting prick were her own. As if the gushing torrent of seed were her victory. At once too full, and growing more drained with every shuddering thrust.

"Giaus—" It was too much. All of it, over-whelming. Her senses heightened to the point of crisis, she was left open to a new world. One that dazed and bewildered and left her vision sparkling with dark stars, her lungs seizing as she shook beneath the on-slaught of his indulgence.

"Take it all," Sinadim snarled, the prince too close and not nearly close enough.

At risk of disembowelment by Giaus' hand...

... and yet, she ached for Sinadim to fill her just as Giaus had. To satisfy some unknown, primitive demand rooted in her very blood and bone. Aching because she could feel him, just there. She could feel the hurt throbbing through his blood before it bled into hers, where a deadly thorn worked itself ever deeper with each hopeless beat of her heart.

Keening, she squirmed and pressed her cheek against the warmth of Sinadim's skin. Trying to soothe the insufferable, cruel prince who hadn't earned what he needed from her. But she couldn't help tasting his scent, taking frantic, shallow breaths against his outer hip. Couldn't stop the ragged sound that spilled over her lips when Giaus snarled and halted her advance.

Jealous, blistering hatred assaulted her senses, and though his fingers were gentle, Giaus was not forgiving. Hands heavy, he pinned her in place and saw that she went no closer to the prince. Instead heating her spine with his nearness, filling her mind and body with him.

Sinadim laughed, but there was a seething darkness there, too. Something insidious that snarled and demanded she yield to his dominance. To shatter, and trust that he would remake her.

She'd been engineered to want that. To be what Sinadim needed in an Omega female, content to be submissive and give up her rebellion at the first whiff of an Alpha male. It was, after all, a carefully selected trait, ingrained over a thousand generations of Hathorians who could pull pleasure from submission, arousal from fear.

And so, when her belly grew taut, ribs hollowed out as her insides flexed, Renegade couldn't help but embrace that fantastic defeat—and was rewarded with an exotic heaviness growing swollen and ripe inside her.

"W-What's happening?" she asked, teeth clacking together as Giaus shuddered and shook. All around her. So terribly deep inside.

"He's going to fuck you pregnant, Omega," Sinadim drawled, watching her from beneath his lashes. Still, but for the blur of his fist and the jerking, desperate muscle rippling at his shoulder cap. "Right now. As I watch."

His voice... deep, cultured and laced with disdain... it made her gush around Giaus' girth. Felt deep in the cradle between her hips, where an alien weight grew plump and more mature with each seasoned touch, every covetous glance or rumbling purr.

Confused tears gathered in her lashes, her sight growing blurry even as her eyes flicked over tiny, insignificant details that held her in rapt fascination despite the males jostling to be the first to tear her in half. Fighting for the privilege of being the one to claim the larger portion.

Utterly bewildered by the rare beauty in the tiniest details, Renegade wept as she was fucked. As her belly grew tighter, overdue for a thing she couldn't name and had never felt before. A thing that needed only the slightest, enticing push...

There was a moment suspended between. Frozen in the void between breaths. Where she was held in thrall by the wispy black hairs framing her own face, floating just outside her field of vision—a stolen instant where she found a symphony written on the wind. A rainbow of dust and debris floating on a gentle breeze, the host of an explosion of color she could taste even without drawing breath.

It couldn't last.

Rupturing, a sharp stab of pain, and she felt pebbles roll free before the dam burst in her core. One after the other, the pebbles were enticed to break away as if summoned into being by the king himself.

"Now!" Sinadim snarled and sucked a hissing breath between his teeth as his balls drew up, parting on either side of his shaft.

Shuddering, Giaus unleashed a powerful knot and seated himself deep. Hooked into place behind her pelvic bone, he roared as he pressed deeper still. Soaking his knot, balls, and the heaps of rumpled bedding as he emptied himself inside her.

Renegade could do little but take it. Panting, drunk on the prickle of fine hairs and sweat slicked against her spine, she tilted her hips up to catch every last drop, just as she was trained to do. Inviting her desecration with a glassy, brittle smile, she felt her lower back bunch and twitch as if the muscles still had a purpose. As if she'd have happily flicked her tail aside and thrown herself at his feet if only he'd be the balm to the thing that ailed her.

"Look at you," Giaus rumbled, and cupped her cheek in one massive hand. Thumb tracing the bladed edge of her opposite jaw, from the corner all the way to her lower lip where it caught and tugged. Letting her taste something salty from the pad of his wandering digit. "*These* tears," he rumbled and laved her cheek so he too might claim a taste. "I find them... pleasing. Perhaps more than even your fire, they suit me."

Offering only a dewy blink and a coo, she hummed a drowsy question.

"I made you sing for me," he replied, testing where they were locked together. Watching as his knot threatened to pull her insides out in a luxurious stretch of intimate flesh. "They are my due. A salty reward for breeding my vicious, wild queen. My mate." He grinned, then. Curling around her to fill every last millimeter of her vision, he pressed a bruising kiss to her lips, and said, "The taste of gravid female is... unrivaled. A delicacy I shall have again and again."

"It's too soon to say," Sinadim said with a mighty yawn. Stretching his arms high above his head, his belly flexing in a show of shivering muscle splattered with ropes of creamy, glistening white. "It takes more than one knot to cross the species barrier, especially for a stubborn thing like her, but..." He shrugged, though she didn't need to see the wicked gleam in his green eye to know the flavor of his jealousy. "I'm sure it's a task you're equal to, my Liege. She won't be going out of season any time soon, after all."

Horror washed over her then. Blanketed by the dense fog that was every fleeting oppressive emotion flicking through the vapid brains of the males smothering the life from her lungs, yet there all the same. And it was then, as she blinked at her surroundings, that Renegade took the time to actually look.

What she saw in the dark was mystifying.

There was Sinadim, lounging alongside them. His belly splashed with ropes of cooling seed that gleamed with shades of pearly blues, blond mane bristling as he offered her a devious smirk and cheeks kissed by the slightest tinge of pink.

Giaus, who refused to be ignored, even for a moment. His long legs sprawled out from one side of a bed she didn't recognize, to the other side of a nest she'd never been in before and hadn't made.

It was a place transformed.

What had once been a dank prison pit had been widened. A gently sloping path carved into the earth, they'd left the back wall high and imposing. Bracketing a nest more glorious than anything she'd seen in Hadim's harem, for it was piled high with every scrap of leather or fur the pack possessed.

Deep and messy, it was a heap of luxury that dominated the burrow. And although not a single thing was in the correct place, its purpose was unmistakable, even through the chaotic disarray.

A nest.

A *true* nest.

One that had been built for her. Around her.

So she might be bred in the way of the ancients.

Fucked pregnant.

Her eyes snapped back to the prince, and she saw his sly smirk for the mask it was. That it concealed a calculating villain playing a far more cerebral game than any she'd thought possible.

One in which she was little more than a fuckable pawn—not the queen of the beyond.

When it started, the shaking came from a chill deep in her bones. Dread, the likes of which she'd never known as a harem Omega. Where she'd been enslaved to Hadim, yes. But she'd been a face among many. Nameless. Lost in the masses. She'd avoided her duty for years.

But here... with two sets of gleaming, feral eyes watching her every insignificant twitch? Her every thoughtless movement? Their noses tipped back to pull each breath through parted lips, licking their chops like the ravenous beasts they really were, beneath it all.

Nausea settled over her. A cold slap. Churning and bubbling behind her palm, where it threatened to boil over.

But then Sinadim grinned, lazy and sure. Hiding sinister motivation beneath his cultured smirk and lowered lashes.

Giaus' jaw flexed against her cheek, the king donning an air of careful nonchalance, while inside he seethed at the nearness of the other male he couldn't slaughter.

Renegade went very still as a single, startling truth made itself known.

They could not feel her.

Inside her heart, a tempest blazed. A festering tsunami of Anhur rage tore into her with a force she'd been utterly unprepared to master. Coming not from one, which alone would have been more than she could safely handle, but from both of the males she'd claimed. Both fighting for dominance, their focus lay not on her, as she smothered beneath the weight of all that toxic, brutal attention... but on each other.

They could not feel her.

No whisper of the terror or the lust. Not a hint of the very real Hathorian fury that she had been chained in this way, to them. Enslaved by her own doing to the very males she'd meant to avoid at all costs. They couldn't feel even a ripple of the excitement building in her heart.

Nothing.

For theirs was a one-sided bond. A tie that afforded the Anhur advantage in almost every category—and left them vulnerable where it mattered most.

Arrogance.

Not exclusive to the Anhur, and yet, it was a quality that would see them undone. A trait that drove them to compete to be the best, have the best, clawing and scratching and fighting for every last scrap of quality breeding female they might take for themselves before they could take no more.

She felt everything.

Knew the distinct flavor of Giaus' possessive devotion. Felt the burn of Sinadim's jealous lust and the tiny flicker of desperate want...

All of it. Hers.

Hers to toy with. To use.

And so instead of cowering, she let her spine go loose. Reveling in the lie, that they could not see what lurked beneath and couldn't hear the whispering doubt that she was not enough. That she was unworthy of naming herself queen.

The nameless harem Omega had been nothing but a vessel.

But *Renegade* was a juggernaut. A proven strategist with more than one victory to her name, she could carry royal bloodlines with ease. By the Nine, she'd named her own king and given him a general as a trusted adviser!

What was she, but a trickster queen who could fool even the mightiest Anhur? A budding master of deception and clever ruses who would see her males fight to distinguish themselves for her pleasure, her attention, and every sordid whim satisfied while she worked in the shadows.

A coy, honeyed smile spread across her lips. Revealing the blunt, smooth edge of gleaming white teeth. "How long?" she murmured, and set her teeth to the king's shoulder without breaking skin. Lining up against the spot where she'd left a silver crescent of scars, teasing the massive male locked inside her, she flicked a cruel glance at the one who'd been denied. "How long has it been?"

"Days," Giaus returned, and she felt that ripple of pride in his words.

But instead of berating, she hummed and tossed a sheet of thick, glossy black hair over her shoulder. Packing the fury neatly away, her smile grew sly when she said, "Impressive stamina worthy of a king."

Giaus, it seemed, had been waiting for her rejection. But at the sound of her praise?

He began to rumble.

Mangled purr rattling through his ribs, he filled her with adoration. Covetous, his instinct was to smother as he cherished. Working at her neck, he kneaded a tight band of muscle bunched around her shoulders. Massaging where she felt irritation shivering in tune with her mood...

A band that didn't exist. Not for her. A Hathorian female who had no mane and could not emote like her infernal mates.

As if to spite her, Giaus shifted. His mane a full, billowing halo about his shoulders, he speared into her all the way to the top of her sodden channel. Seating that bloated girth deep as it could go, he said, "Anything to please my vicious mate," and sluiced through the mess he'd made. Something soft gleamed in golden eyes. Something precious that made all sorts of uncomfortable promises she had no intention of claiming.

Cracking her neck with a deep sigh, she cast a teasing glance over her shoulder and said, "I am your *queen*." Lips teasing and playful where they crinkled at the edges, instead of submission she offered a smile. "And I have had enough of underground, windowless vaults."

At this, Giaus lunged. Pressing a brutal

kiss to swollen lips, he breathed a drugging purr straight into her lungs. "*Yes.* My vicious, precious Renegade Queen. There is much to be seen. Much that has been done in reward for your suffering."

Humming low in her throat, Renegade glanced at Sinadim and plied him with a coy pass of her tongue. "Then impress me."

Detangling them from the heap of soiled furs, Giaus' fingers held her spread where she was locked in place atop his knot. Back to front, he turned as if she weighed nothing in his arms, his every ground-eating stride taking them further from the nest he'd built around her.

He didn't stop until they stood at the mouth of the den, overlooking her budding domain. Sinadim warming her right side, he waited just a half stride back.

A breath of fresh air slid over heated, sweat-slicked skin. Refreshing, despite the wave of gooseflesh that followed, granting enough clarity that she could look without pain.

It was night.

The Queen's Landing lit by a dozen torches she avoided in favor of the shadows they cast.

Gone were the corpses of the damned. Their blood and gore washed away as if they'd never been. The only hint of the carnage was the oily black stains of a cremation fire still smoldering at the forest's edge. Downwind and downstream.

The forest itself had been pushed well back. Saplings felled in an impressive radius, and while some had undoubtedly fueled the fires, the rest had been whittled into spears that ringed the red stone clearing two rows deep.

"Behold," Giaus said and slipped one massive hand between them. Compressing the base of his knot, he unleashed a gushing flood of seed and set her on her feet. "The Queen's Landing."

Straightening, Renegade eyed the landing with keen interest, eyes flicking over every new feature. Each budding construction project where hybrids toiled to build a fortress in the wild.

Seeking an escape. A weakness that might be exploited.

Anything at all she could use to take the one and only thing she'd ever asked for.

Freedom.

But the time to claim her vengeance, her chance, would come—but only when the Anhur had been mollified. Given exactly what they expected of a Hathorian female, and were in turn sedated by her obedience.

So instead of seething, she smiled. Where she might have screamed her throat bloody, she purred, wanting nothing so much as she wanted to run.

And then her demeanor shifted, became almost coy as she glanced at her king from beneath the fan of thick dark lashes. Clapping her hands, Renegade said, "A perfect place to build an army so we might challenge the Silver City and claim what is owed."

Giaus went rigid. Posturing, his mane standing on end as a shiver of delight skated down his back.

It was Sinadim who glared, the former prince who knew not to trust something so sweet.

The ghost of her tail flicking, Renegade sashayed away from the mouth of the den. Shunned the fresh air and that tender glimpse of freedom, and retreated into the gloom without a backward glance.

"Cut down the trees," she ordered. "Build me a wall no horde can climb, and then we shall speak of breeding. And by the embers of Toth, this den is dank and dreary!" she called from the dark. "Filth in every corner. Clean this up, or I'll paint the walls with murder."

At her back, Giaus laughed. Filling her heart with mirth, he said, "It shall be done," through a purr.

And she smiled, despite the circumstances.

For she had a secret.

One that was all her own, that she'd keep close to her breast. A coveted scrap not meant for the Anhur.

And with sensitive pupils fixed into the dark, ears pricked forward, she said, "Oh, and light some torches."

16

Sinadim blinked.

Jaws hanging slack, he watched Renegade turn as if in a swirl of silks. Regal in the way she whirled and shot a lurid glance over her shoulder. Beckoning. Lower back bunching where her tail might have flicked in invitation, she turned *away* from the clearing. Shunned the breath of fresh air, and returned to her den.

"*You* want a wall?" he asked, incredulous. "You? The female I couldn't hold in a den of her own choosing?" Long legs gobbling up the space between them, he stalked her shadow as she led him deeper into the dark —a dark she wanted lit with torches. "A harem Omega who escaped her duty to Hadim, denied my royal bloodline, refused the protection of a pack, and named herself *Renegade—you* want a wall?"

She watched him from beneath a fan of dark lashes, lips crinkled ever so slightly.

Gold gleaming where her irises reflected what little light there was in her dank and dreary nest. "I'm certain my king is capable of single-handedly defending us," she murmured. "But it seems a bit arrogant to invite the next horde in, wouldn't you say? Correct me if I'm wrong, *general*, but it seems the wiser course of action to erect an obstacle or two between us and them, hmm?"

Incredulous, Sinadim looked to Giaus and found the king standing rigid in her wake. Unblinking, he bristled and postured for the attention of a female he couldn't stop watching. One he *already* possessed.

"Giaus... This is a trick!" Sinadim said, whirling. His claws flashing, he snapped forefinger and thumb to break Giaus' line of sight. "It's a distraction and a bad one at that."

Giaus lifted one massive, burly shoulder and craned his neck to look around Sinadim. "She'll have her torches and her wall," he said, resuming his watchful vigilance. "And if she runs, I shall have my hunt."

A moment passed between king and queen. Heavy with meaning that excluded Sinadim. "Mmm," she purred, and her eyes flashed a reflective, devious green. "My king wields my authority."

Head thrown back, Giaus coughed up a barking laugh. Mirth echoing through a voice deep enough to recall the wisdom of the ancients.

And despite the pang of hurt, Sinadim

threw up his hands, and said, "Fine!" because there was something far greater to be gained in this moment. A chit called on a favor already claimed—and he would not be denied another instant. "Then I'll take what I am owed before she runs again."

Tinkling laughter tickled his ears, and Sinadim spun. Fixing his good eye upon the creature backing into the sunken pit where the dregs of a nest awaited.

"Why would I run?" she asked, ears laid out to either side. Taunting even as she enticed. *Confident* in the way she watched him and didn't blink as the shadows wrapped about her thin shoulders and embraced. Her smirk both fierce and defiant in just the way that made his cock throb. "I'm to be cherished," she drawled. "Served by my king *and* my general... Something precious, guarded from theft... or escape." And then, gracing him with a small, sad little smile she shrugged. "I had to try, remember? I failed. And now I'm left to salvage what I can."

A tiny puff of held breath misted over Sinadim's lips. His words echoed back to haunt him as his mate turned. Knowing he would follow.

At this, she sank back into the nest, and he caught the moment that her attention faltered. Where she transitioned from budding queen to nesting Omega. A female who couldn't help but twist in worn leathers, turning and turning and turning again, until she found comfort in an act shunned in the Silver City. Primitive and messy, that of commoners who'd let an Omega go into heat without the aid of suppressors to keep her civilized.

But this was the Feral Court.

The Renegade Queen was already in her nest, already saturated with the scents of Anhur musk she couldn't ignore.

And for just a moment, Sinadim resisted the urge to scatter all that she had placed just so—ignored the bulge of an eager knot swelling at his base. Content to bear witness to the ancient ritual, this instinct that had consumed her. For despite the many nameless Omegas Sinadim had once boasted... he'd never had Renegade. Never allowed a female to lead, just to see where she might take him.

Swallowing a lump lodged at the back of his throat, Sinadim bristled when she stretched. Throwing both arms over her head, she tilted her chin back, nipples jutting up. Peaked and beaded, they begged for attention as she arched to reveal the languid bend of hollow ribs—and an empty cradle between her hips.

His resistance shattered at the sight, for that was his price. The value of his fealty, the bid to retain his expert-fucking-counsel the king needed but didn't want. And the very last secret of keeping Hathorian females he had left to divulge—that in breeding an

Omega in the throes of a natural cycle, *without suppressants*, timing was crucial. The act one that required practice...

... or a guide.

And now Giaus had everything.

Sinadim had... *this*.

A chance to share the litter Giaus may well have pumped into her this night. That he too might plant life inside her and know the secret joy of seeing his own eyes staring back at him in a face he recognized and had only just met.

"Come," she murmured and flashed the straight edge of blunt teeth. "You have a promise to keep."

Mane shivering with scarcely contained lust, Sinadim lifted one brow. "Is that so?"

"You said you'd come so deep inside, you wouldn't have to bother with a knot." She hummed. Moving to cup her breasts, worrying at her nipples as her eyes were dragged down. Drawn by the way his cock jerked, a pulse of silky want beading at his tip. "Promised it would take a week for me to stop dripping."

At this, Giaus made his presence known. Vibrating, seething with contempt Sinadim could literally taste, the king's brow grew damp with the evidence of his temper. His restraint.

"I want that," Renegade cooed, oblivious to the war she insisted on feeding, an evil little grin spreading across her lips. Spurred on by the way Giaus blustered at the edge of her nest.

"You're going to get me murdered," Sinadim replied, leery of the beast rumbling with a low, threatening growl. Bristling with the sort of possessive madness only a few Anhur ever had the chance to know. The sort only soothed with the attention of a willing female.

Forcing his mane to go flat, his scent muted, posture meek, Sinadim turned his cheek.

Exposing his silver eye to the king.

Giving up the place where he was most vulnerable, where he wouldn't see that final mercy coming until it was much too late.

It was a subtle concession of trust, and it was enough.

Though Giaus' glare only narrowed and he reeked of heat and musk, he issued a guttural chuff and made no move to interfere.

Sinadim did not need a second invitation.

Surging into the nest, he fell to his knees. Scooping both hands over Renegade's thighs, palms traveling up until his hands and claws anchored where her ribs tucked neatly in.

"Roll," he barked and took himself in hand. Greedy in the way he took in her every inch of naked flesh. Pumping his shaft and pulling yet another laced breath through his teeth, so he might taste her in the way only he and Giaus could.

Dainty hands found a place on either side

of his belly button. Thumbs sweeping up and around, she slowed his frantic pace without bothering to speak a word. Lifting a single brow, she let her knees fall apart.

And smiled through her denial.

Helpless but to obey, his eye fell to what lay between.

"By the Nine," he rasped and swallowed, *hard*. Marveling at the sight. Mouth watering as frilled, glistening petals spread for his pleasure, glimmering in the shadows where he could only just see them.

Torches were a fine idea. Crucial, even, for their continued survival. He'd have them struck, mounted, and lit before the hour was out, even if he had to do it himself.

Just so he could sit and marvel at all that was golden and precious.

Slick.

His to do with as he pleased.

A tap that would never run dry. Her season never-ending, she alone could replace his harem of hundreds—*and* give herself to Giaus without running herself aground.

He'd seen it too many times, through the opposite lens. What the skin traders did to force Hathorian females to accommodate their Anhur mates. Forced to breed, they'd take any who appeared between their legs and begged until their voices grew weak and brittle.

Squeezing his eyes shut, claws threatening to shred his palms, he shuddered.

Frothing hatred threatened to bubble up, torrid memories working to shatter his tightly held composure. Breath frozen in his lungs, he sealed his lips and tried to forget the dreadful dead littering his past. Scarcely able to look upon her face for all it evoked... But neither could he look away.

He was tormented by the past, engaged to the future and whatever it might hold.

"Do you hate me that deeply?"

The question made him lurch. Eyes snapping open, he stared at down at her and looked at the creature he'd traded everything just to touch.

Hate her?

Hate her?

Sweating, Sinadim pulled a breath between his lips, painted the little idiot's scent along the roof of his mouth, and in an instant, he was consumed. Thrown fully into that divine Sight, he took one slender thigh in trembling, clawed fingers, and draped it over his shoulder. Diving between her legs, where she wept for his attention, that of her *mate*, he tasted what had been denied him for too long.

Color exploded all around him. Bringing shadows to life, he groaned deep in his chest. The sound pulled up from the very bottom of his being. A place he'd thought long buried was exposed to the expanse of inky dark pupils blown wide and ringed in gold. Cracked open so she could feel every twisted, horrific ounce of him while he worshipped and showed her what he hid in the dark.

Her breath caught. Stuttered as he made a lurid sweep of delicate petals. Teased with his teeth and lips.

Icy flames shivered through his blood. Leaving his mane standing on end, his lower back bunched where his tail had been and wasn't. He let his tongue flick back so he might drink her as deep as he could. Losing himself to the rut, knowing that too she was helpless beneath him. Willing... eager.

That she *felt* him, as no other might.

Everything he couldn't possibly name. All of it, hers.

"Yesss," she hissed and trapped him there between her thighs. Heels locked behind his neck, her fingers twisting at his temples. Holding him in place as she positioned him exactly where she needed him. Taking, as only a queen might, she fed him every drop of that creamy want.

He drank. Eager for the rush of the taboo, that he should want this one female to such an absurd degree.

His precious mate.

Sinadim glanced up and saw the silver ends of scars marking her inner elbow.

Scars that matched, lining up with the mirrored defects that had obliterated his face and ruined his eye.

Reminding him what this precious, im-possible creature had suffered just to be here.

What she had endured—the wilds... exile... *Hadim.*

She had been blighted by the cruelty of the Silver City, just as he had.

More, for he'd been a prince before he'd been a general.

And she... she had been Hadim's.

Groaning as he dined on ambrosia, Sinadim slipped one hand back and worked himself all the way to the edge. Balls growing heavy, flexing with the urge to pump her full. To breed her, because she was ripe. Here. His.

Theirs.

Using his every unfair advantage to please his mate. Just to watch her dance for him, he played on the edge of an orgasm because he knew how it would set her ablaze and he wanted to watch her dance at his behest.

Slick gushed forth, wetting his lips and chin as tension wound her muscles tight as they might go. She trembled at his command. This impossible queen he shared with a beast.

The thought spawned a savage thing to unfurl in his chest. One that saw Renegade gasp, her pupils liquid pools of seething, ravenous black.

It was merely a reflection.

One mirrored from the tempest raging in his heart. Cock an aching band of steel that begged for attention, he pumped as he feasted. Once, twice, milking himself until a bead of pearly lust burst from his slit where his knob peeked between the circle of his fingers. A drop of desperate want captured on the pad of his thumb, only to be sent through sodden folds an instant later. Spreading her with that laced digit, he exposed the bundle of swollen nerves, pulled her clit between his lips, and sucked.

Hard.

Thighs quaking, Renegade came undone. Clenching and thrashing, her back bowed, thumping into the furs as she gave up that liquid gold.

And an instant before her eyes rolled back, her lips parted on a poisoned barb that shredded the thin veil of sanity he'd clung to all his life.

A nickname uttered in ecstasy, she tried to call out his name and instead, found his deepest most painful memory.

"Sina!"

17

"**S**ina!"

Wailing long and low, he watched her pace a ragged line, mewling for help. Reaching as the guards took aim, ruined fingers mangled by the virus lifted in a pitiful salute before the spears began to fall...

A breathless howl of madness ruptured the fabric between past and present. A sound that came from Sinadim's own lips. Denied too long, the rut flooded in. Consuming everything in its path, a monster was born between spread thighs.

Any hint of cultured civility was ripped away.

Replaced by a savage.

A snarling heathen who abandoned his meal in favor of marking it as his own. Primal, that urge. To plunge into the depths of his mate and stain her with his scent. His seed.

His sons.

Mane standing on end, reeking of aggression, he surged into her and pressed a snarl under her chin. Lips ghosting over her pulse, just so he might taste her where she was frantic. Where the tendon between shoulder and neck was bow-tight.

"Do it," she rasped, goading when she should have guarded that spot for another.

But Sickle was dead.

Fucking him from below, she worked his length with a divine cunt. Rippling along his shaft, she set her lips to his temple. A whispered, "Impress me, Sina," stabbing him straight through the heart.

And without meaning to, he snarled, "*You will not call me that!*" and caught her throat in a cage of claws that dimpled that fine alabaster skin. Dragging her thighs over his hips, one after the other, he sheathed his throbbing prick. Over and over again, bullying his way inside, desperate to find her end and crash against it, he bucked into her depths. Howled when she arched beneath him—*toward* him—that tight sheath grew warm and impossibly slick.

Welcoming her destruction with a smile.

Ears laid out, she trapped him in an inky pitch that yawned wide and swallowed him whole. Looped golden chains about his throat and twisted her fingers in his dense, blond mane. Pulling him close, she pressed her lips to his ear, and said, "You belong to me." And then, cupping the cheek ridged with scars that no longer wept or itched, she smiled. "My darkest Sin. My Eye who sees the way through."

Obeying the slightest flick of obsidian eyes rimmed in gold, the shadows moved at her command—and the warning came too late.

One thick, burly forearm slid beneath his chin. Hauling back on his neck until stars sparkled where his vision was black.

Searing, prickling heat ground against his spine. The expanse of his back, one jagged hip bone striking him where his tail wasn't.

Giaus.

"Everything you to do her..." A breath rattled against his ear as the weight of a colossus fell across his back. "... I will do to you."

The bulge of taboo intention pulsed against his thigh. Sticky... wet.

Hard.

"She is *mine!*" the general howled, fucking into sodden heat. "My absolution. My freedom. I have to drink! I have to—she is *life!* An offense to the Nine to waste even a drop, to let it spill without a knot. This is my price, mutant king! That you let me quench my thirst, cleansed from the outside in. Every gulp of perfect, honeyed gold"—he snarled and choked against that forearm, mane shivering, hips working—"a tribute to the Nine for their divine gift of Sight."

Giaus coughed up a barking laugh that puffed against the general's shoulder. "Are you not indulged? Your price paid. You rut into my mate, even now, *Sin*."

Desperate to lose himself with the female wrapped tight about his cock, Sin's hips worked a frantic rhythm that could not be stopped. Not for beauty or beast or a whisper of self-preservation. "Giaus—"

"I have accepted this... arrangement," Giaus drawled, and Sin felt the words against his cheek, even through the edges of madness. The loathing and the distaste of the admission. "That I cannot provide all that she needs. And when she pleads for a knot," he murmured, reeking of hoppy musk and futile temper that would find an outlet, "*Both* of us will have to suffice."

Sluicing through a mess of frothed ambrosia, Sin fell. His mind taken by a primal frenzy. Rabid. Entranced by the languid depths of that glassy ebon stare...

... enticed by something... darker.

Something simply not done.

Giaus reached and pressed his shaft down. Over the crease of swinging balls, smearing against the vein that fed Sin's knot, and stilled. Letting the general's own helpless rhythm paint his monstrous length in mercy.

Slick as lubrication.

Renegade mewled against Sin's throat, nursing at the mark she'd left on his shoulder. Pressing little possessive kisses to the heat of his skin, she said, "Be my general. My advisor who sees all. My Eye."

Drunk on the rut, on the thrill of competition and the helpless little quiver that melted through the mania to send a whisper of pure lust winding through his blood and lungs, Sin shivered. Setting his knees in the nest, braced wider, so he might open her for a deeper, more thorough breeding, he pressed his brow to hers. Damp with sweat.

And nodded.

Tight.

Just once.

Accepting all of it.

Giaus' forearm fell away, and with a lazy confidence, the giant reset the blunt end of that threatening girth.

Teeth grinding, jaw clenching around the desperate, titillating fear, he allowed himself to stare into those languid pools of inky black rimmed in gold. To lose himself in the moment. Fully.

Beneath him, a female that was far from helpless. One wrapped around him as he bucked into welcoming heat.

At his back, the weight of another male. The slide of muscle, the bruising grip—the burn of a stretch he'd only dared to wonder about.

Pulse thrashing at the base of his throat, he shuddered as Giaus pressed and made him burn. As he opened for the king, *and could not stop rutting the queen.*

"Fuck him, Sin," Renegade whispered and

nipped at his lips. "Take him inside and fuck us both."

He did.

Breath hitching, he did as she bade. Grinding as deep as she could take, he indulged his knot.

Pulling back, he rocked onto a spear of flesh made slippery with slick. The passage easier than he would have ever thought possible. Burning with the ache for more as it battered and stretched.

Harder.

Deeper.

He only barreled forward when the terror of being impaled by that monstrosity spilled over, and so was rewarded with Renegade.

He withdrew when he grew bold and daring, and so was punished by Giaus.

"Fuck," he rasped, back arching as he rocked to and fro. Slippery front to back, bewildered by sweat and limbs and a tight glove overfull with another's cock.

Mewling, Renegade didn't bother herself to wait. She came, gushing, her legs quivering with the violence of it, and Sin was taken by the sounds drawn from her throat.

One clawed fist darted between his legs. A horrible flashback that delayed his own spillage, until Giaus laughed. "Frightened little prince," he drawled and bore down. Filling him all the way to the top of his knot, the king began to work when Renegade's eyes rolled back. Fucking him without violence, because she could feel it.

Groaning, Sin felt Giaus' shaft thicken even as it pummeled. "Shit," he hissed and went still. Buried inside one mate as the other bred him from the back. Forced him to feel the edge of a building knot, and wonder if he'd be made to take that too.

Helpless but to endure the power of another's rut.

A sordid moan escaped his lips, then. As he indulged the wonder that was a Hathorian embrace... that another male was about to fuck him into an absolutely titanic orgasm. Shameless, for he had no more secrets to suffer for.

Not here, where his obsessive want was tempered by a king. Contained by a queen.

Three savage strokes and Giaus succumbed with a grunt and yards of shuddering muscle. Buried deep, he made sure Sin felt every kicking pulse. The flex of swollen balls growing unburdened as he emptied himself inside Sin's bowels—and spared him the cruelty of his knot.

And then, panting along the back of his neck, Giaus let go that royal sack and unleashed a tsunami. Uttering a commanding chuff that rattled through his skull and found a quiver in his balls.

Untethered, Sin roared, vision sparkling as he gave everything he had for his chance to breed the queen. "Take it," he rasped and set his knot behind the ledge of her pelvic bone. Rocking gently through her slick and lathered walls. "Please. *Please.*"

"Begging now?" Giaus panted and eased back. Careful now that the moment had cooled. Leaving Sin to be milked inside that clenching Hathorian sheath. "Frightened that she might reject an unworthy mate?"

Sin hushed the king. "She'll hear you, my *Liege.*" And then, when it was clear that she was beyond hearing, he uttered a hoarse chuckle, rolling so he could adjust Renegade where she was impaled and knotted on his lap. Letting her slumber, his claws carding through sweat-damp black silk. "Self-preservation," he said at length. And then, "She'll kill us both if she finds out."

To this, Giaus hummed, but that was all.

And for a moment, as a comfortable, satisfied silence fell over the trio, Sin thought he saw the glimmer of something gold flash in the queen's eyes. Thought he'd felt her tense, where a moment before she'd been boneless across his chest.

But he couldn't see in the dark and wasn't sure.

"Torches," Sin murmured through a yawn. "She wants torches."

And then, lounging in their nest, he pressed one palm to the velvet cone of her outer ear, took a shallow breath, and exhaled life into twitching muscles he'd never used before. Letting his breath hum through his sinuses, a haunting melody bubbled up. A song for the death queen who'd given him life. It was a passion he'd never known, devotion to a delicate creature he'd spend the rest of his life cherishing in the way only a Sultan's son might.

A general who'd been a prince, unafraid to purr for his queen.

18

Three times the moons had waxed.

Three times they'd waned as she'd watched the Queen's Landing transform from a simple riverside clearing into a fortress.

A wall ringed their den in safety. Designed to her exact specifications, it stood twenty feet above her head. Any tree tall enough to fall and become a ladder for an infected wanderer was felled in a circumference around the wall.

And there, built atop a great outdoor dining room, they'd erected a turret twice the height of the wall—where they could see an enemy coming and act before their doom was through the gates.

Renegade had ordered it done with a smile.

Watched as the points of entry—or escape—were whittled down to two. Both were under constant, careful observation by a litany of males with senses unrivaled by even the very best Anhur hunter the Silver City had *ever* boasted.

Escape from males who could see her every wayward step outlined in shimmering lines of painted gold? It couldn't be done.

Affecting an air of blissful contentment, that of a well-bred Omega whose every sordid need had been met, Renegade let them see a female who slept in the same den night after night. She became a queen who greeted her males when they returned from a hunt and let them feed her choice cuts from beasts she didn't have to kill herself. Males who never let her stomach growl. To whom spears were tools, not a means of desperate survival. Free to come and go at will, as long as they obeyed the laws of their new king.

By the time the triplet moons had waned for the third time, Renegade's hard edges had softened once more. Her rangy muscle not needed for the life of a pampered queen reigning in the heart of a fledgling civilization, serene behind those walls where her primary duty was to catch Anhur seed and let it grow.

Kept safe from what lurked in the untamed wilds, no matter how seductive the call.

All of it an illusion.

Exactly what they wanted to see, it was a mask she wore with practiced ease. One disguising a crackling inferno that might only be tempered by vengeance for what they'd done. To her. Her people. To this fledgling society in the beyond for which they'd sat her on a pedestal named *Hope*, without bothering to mention it was rotten all the way through.

Her ears flicked back, but only for an instant before she caught herself. Before she concealed the irate twitch beneath a show of distracted grooming. Mussing the silky tresses Giaus had perfected only minutes before.

Gaze wandering to the wall and beyond, she pulled a black fur cloak tighter about her shoulders and sat at the threshold of her den. Feet dangling in the swirling pools of her private baths, she watched the sun give way to her beloved moons. And there, at the corner of her lips, a tiny secret smile. Her eyes liquid and glassy as she squinted through the dying light so she might catch just a glimpse of the woods beyond the wall.

In her fingers, a snarl of forest dander Sin had brought from their last hunt. Bits of detritus and pretty things for her nest. A burrow she'd learned to tend from an Anhur prince who knew more of Hathorian culture than she'd ever dreamed could possibly exist. Who watched her most carefully of all, one green eye tracking her every twitch, he waited for her act to fail, for the tempest to crack through. Waited for his turn to mount her in the nest he'd helped her build, so he might piss off the king and find his every taboo, lewd desire satiated.

Giaus had taught her to use her new senses. Their one-sided bond thrumming with joy as he showed her what it was to see through his eyes. With his Sight. Delighting in every new scent she experienced as if for the first time. Each new taste that touched the dimples now lining the roof of her mouth. Murmuring devotions against the velvet cone of her ear as he fucked her placid. His stamina was a thing of legend, rivaled only by Sin's tolerance for denial and punishment.

But not once in all that time did the king think to so much as ask her if his sight was the *only* thing she saw.

Anhur arrogance was her advantage.

She was changed.

Feral.

A creature born of artful lies biding her time until her moment materialized.

One who hid in plain sight. Coiled and ready, a predator they thought leashed and tamed.

It had taken them weeks to let her wander the compound. Months to do so unattended, despite the height of the wall and the guards at the exits.

She glanced up, to the top of the wall separating the Queen's Landing from the wilds of the great beyond. Knowing she couldn't scale it without being caught. That to risk her thin veneer of civility for an imperfect moment was to botch everything she'd worked so hard to attain.

She'd needed their trust so she could have their complacency. So they might see her daily perimeter walks as nothing suspicious, and desensitize the hypersensitive.

What was disguised beneath the illusion of a well-bred queen, merely waited to lash out before it was too late. Before her fire smothered beneath the devotion heaped on her from her mates.

Before all that she was... was lost. Swallowed up and divided between males who knew better than she how she liked her meals. When to drink. When to fuck and fight and breathe and andand*and*—

Their bond was sick. Too much for them, too little for her. All that remained siphoned off to feed something new.

Renegade was withering as she screamed and begged and wept for them to see her. To give something back, feed her spirit before it was nothing but embers.

And she'd done it to herself. All of it, by her own orders.

Before long, this compound, and all that went with it, would make her... happy.

She couldn't help the sneer any more than she could help the way her eyes tracked the moons that frolicked across that expanse of welcoming black.

Anhur thrived in the blinding heat, happiest in the cruel glare of the midday sun, while she watched through slitted eyes from the shadows. Squinting against the day. Unbearably drowsy until the night was upon them.

And then...

She smiled, for she and the night were old friends. Lovers who shared explosive secrets no one else could see.

Head tilted back, Renegade inhaled and fell into the Sight she shared with her Anhur. Tasting the wind, so she might see despite the sun still hanging low on the horizon. For without the Sight painting scents around shapes she could see... she was almost blind in the day. Everything washed out by eyes better suited for low light. Meant for the shadows where her kind were born and raised.

All it took was a moment. A single accidental instant of distraction and her moment grew ripe enough to pluck.

It happened at dusk.

As she was pacing the shadows at the wall, admiring the broad shoulders of gleaming, sweat-damp muscles toiling in the clearing below.

One of the twins dropped a hank of meat into a pot of oil heating on the cooking fire—overfilled, it boiled over in seconds and sent rendered fat directly into the flames.

Fire leapt at the chance to feast, sending her hissing back, forearm thrown over her eyes as she hid from the searing pain assaulting her retinas.

And so it was, by chance, that Renegade found herself staring at the open gate as every available male rushed to douse the flames.

It was nothing to wander just a little... closer.

Not something she really even meant to do. It was instinct to answer that call. To find the thing she was missing. To discover why, with two mates stuffed inside her head and her cunt, she felt unbearably... *lonely.*

Inspecting what lay on the other side of that wall, Renegade saw the forest teeming with savage life that called to her from the shadows and her lips curled around a secret smile.

The decision was easy.

The opportunity ripe.

And without pausing to overthink, the queen seized her moment. Took advantage of Micha's lapse in attention and slipped through the open gate. Ignoring the sparkle of pain from a severed tail that had never healed quite right, she fled. Pouring everything she had into her escape, she slipped into the Sight with a sigh. Letting glittering trails of scent pull her wherever they might until the sun set and her vision adjusted.

For when the dark reigned, she had no need of Giaus' eyes or his Sight.

She was Omega.

Exactly what her ancestors had suffered to produce.

Born to conquer. Made to endure.

When the triplet moons reigned, her Hathorian eyes showed her divinity.

All around her, the night lit with a thousand, *thousand* colors. Unspeakable beauty singing a language she was desperate to learn. Not for the mates she'd taken, whose constant, stifling presence had all but smothered the fires from her very soul. Not for the Nine who'd never bothered to grant her favor.

For her.

Wandering, her pace leisurely when she could no longer hear the shouts for water as her males worked to douse the flames, she stopped to press her face into a night bloom. One that glittered with thrice the brilliance of the stars, flickering and dancing under the moonlight. A velvet shade of purple she just had to touch—that shifted to magenta where her fingerprints disturbed a fine coating of pollen. Reflecting the dim light in a different direction.

Delighted, Renegade shivered and slapped the flower just to send the pollen into the wind. A gentle breeze that shimmered and danced, sparkling in the low light that to her, had the look of myth. Colors so deep and rich, so beautiful in their depth, that she blinked back tears. Enthralled by the swirling fantasy she found in the night.

Her attention was snagged by a mushroom cap, and she spun off course. It was the biggest she'd ever seen, her equal in height. On its dewy cap, a shade of red she'd never known before. Striking. Unique.

Deadly.

It was a warning, she knew. One that promised consequences should she dare a nibble.

Compelled to touch without tasting, she ran greedy fingers over the doughy surface. Marveling at the way the skin gave beneath her fingers.

A grunt from behind was the only whisper that her dalliance with the dark had been interrupted. The only warning of danger, and without thinking, she crouched low. Ears tucked flat, she darted clear of something heavy that whistled before it made the glittering pollen scatter. Cleaving the sparkling wind in half where she'd been standing only an instant before.

Claws sliced through the mushroom and sent a cloud of green spores exploding into the night. Sap sprayed across the queen's face —blurring her vision with the tint of toxic green.

Barely a hair separated her from a gruesome death.

And when she blinked and saw what it was that hunted her, her jaws went slack.

It wasn't real.

Couldn't be.

The horror was too vibrant to be anything more than a mushroom-induced hallucination.

A lump of half-sentient flesh and deformed bone that heaved for breath. Mutated beyond all recognition, except where hair bristled in a rough imitation of a mane, it was a nightmare walking. One that huffed and groaned, rattling in some hideous rendition of a growl. Heavy jaws stretched wide enough to swallow her legs all the way up to her navel and still draw breath, it rippled as she watched.

Tendons snapping, it hauled that heavy club up, back, letting her see where flesh had been stretched too thin over muscles that had grown at an unbelievable pace. She could plainly see arteries and veins through that papery skin, red and blue ropes that had grown thick enough that she could plug one with the tip of her finger and still have room to wriggle.

Bile splashed the back of her throat as she darted to the left—and saw a thing that stole her breath.

A single watery blue eye. Glassy. Pupils skating between a tiny prick of seething black, and widely blown.

Claiming slow millimeters of blue as that pupil yawned wide and swallowed everything that she'd been in a single greedy gulp. Twitching in the socket, it rolled toward her, beaming with hateful accusation.

A poor attempt at a smile spread over sagging lips. Drooping heavily on the left side, this mask was a mockery of a face she'd loved, once. Before she'd been a queen.

The beast rumbled as it hefted its bulk another step closer.

Renegade's feet slid apart. And she let the horror of her past slip away with a wet splat, stiffening her spine even as she braced. "I'll do better," she murmured, a eulogy whispered too late to offer comfort to any but herself. "For the others. Our sisters... our daughters. For the matrons who guide us and all who come next. *Better*. That's what this feral court is. A chance for more. And..." The queen's throat flexed around an ache, but despite the urge, she didn't fight the sob. Fought to truly feel the tears as they ran hot and salty down her cheeks. "And I'm sorry."

Groaning, making a terrible mess of the grotto, the beast planted one grotesquely mutated arm and struck the earth with a hollow thud. Fetid breath foaming and spitting, its hideous skull tipped to one side.

"Balkazar?" Renegade gasped because, in the right light, it was obvious. "By the Nine..." she said, too shocked to do more than gape at what the war chief had become.

And there was something about the way his single eye had fixed to her face. Something in the manner he pulled a breath through sagging jaws and let his tongue flick back... along the roof of his mouth.

Tasting her...

... for he was *Giaus'* creation.

Not hers.

Swallowing back the terror, the queen stood before the monster and let him take her in with senses he'd inherited from a line that would be noble. Fought to ignore the urge to submit, to turn tail and flee into the welcoming dark, she allowed him to fall into the Sight and see just how far above him she perched.

This grievance between them needed an ending, unsavory as it was.

"Mmmm," the beast moaned, huffing at the place where she'd been. His monstrous jaws sagging as he panted and drank the wind. "Tassssste..." Lurching, Balkazar lifted one clumsy club, peering down at her as he tried to aim a mass far too heavy to wield with anything resembling accuracy.

Wanted another taste, did he?

Feet planted, knuckles dirty with the glitter of rich, dark soil, she reached for the tie binding her cloak about her shoulders. Not daring so much as a blink as the beast bothered itself to close the distance between them.

But still, she waited.

Relaxed, if ready.

Waiting for the truth to penetrate that thick, mutated skull.

Knowing she could out-pace what had once been a formidable Anhur before he'd become... *this.*

Ugly. Only half as hideous in death as he'd been in life.

For a moment, he did nothing but pant for breath. Balancing a weight that should not have been as he glared down at her. Murder gleamed bright and furious from that ring of icy blue.

Hatred.

Loathing for all that she was. What she'd been born into... that she'd never be *his.*

It was a cancer not of his own doing, this blanket of disgust he held for Hathorians. Something vile that plagued the Silver City, a corruption that had ultimately led to his fall.

And as they stared at each other—a relic and the dawning of something new—she felt nothing for the male who'd earned every tumor. Every weeping, hideous pustule.

But he didn't strike.

Frozen, that icy blue eye had widened with shock as he stared. Painting her scent along the roof of his mouth.

Again.

And again. And again and over again.

And then he dropped to his knees with a strangled horrendous sob. Trembling. Trying to lift hooked and disfigured claws toward her, to touch with careful knuckles, a sound scratching over distorted vocal cords.

"*Mmmpinnnce*," he moaned and thumped his clubbed fist over three distinct ridges of scar tissue marking his chest. "*Mmmmpince*."

It was a truth she'd been trying to ignore. A hidden peek of soft swells revealed beneath her heavy cloak when she stood before him without fear. Nightdress clinging to her skin as if kissed by the gentle breeze.

The whisper of change on the wind, growing in her blood. An ember that would start an inferno and burn away all the relics that couldn't adapt.

It was a serene image, but a perfect metaphor for everything that defined what she'd become. No longer Hathorian, she was something... new.

It was then, as the old world knelt and offered tribute, that she found she didn't need an apology for the horrors of the past.

For with Giaus' Sight, she caught a faint glimmer of her future. A taste that shimmered in her mind and sang of completion and desperate, aching glorious need. Ambrosia that was ripe for the taking, if only she'd reach out and pluck it from the vine.

The trail of something slight that had once flown through this wood, as she had. To claim independence from the Anhur and find the secrets meant for those who'd inherit the night.

Taking flight, the queen was gone before

what was left of Balkazar could open his eye
or attempt to speak another cursed word.

The only sign of her passing was a heap
of black fur, forgotten in the detritus.

Her cloak.

The beast fell, feasting without bothering
to kill...

19

Swiping soot from his brow, Giaus blinked back a scowl that gleamed amber in the dying light of flickering flames. Not trusting even the torches that lit their compound after spending half the night fighting flames.

"By the Nine, that was close," Sin murmured, shaking out a charred fur they'd used to extinguish the inferno. One he'd taken straight from their nest. "Make a note for future reference, eh? Do *not* overfill the oil pot, and only water an oil fire if you want to burn to death in flames that won't die and spread faster than venereal disease through a war camp. Shit."

Giaus chuckled. "Duly noted." And then, "Let Renegade know she can come out now. Fire's out. Oh," he added, sneering. Not bothering to smother the flare of his mane. "And douse the fucking torches in the nest."

Spitting into the embers, Sin nodded,

glaring at a blister on his knuckles. "Think she'll ever admit the light hurts her eyes, or do we just go on pretending not to notice for the rest of time?"

"Let her keep her secrets," Giaus returned, knowing what it meant to the fierce little thing. To have something that was totally her own, untainted by... them. "They're harmless enough."

But he couldn't help it.

That he'd been made for her.

That he needed to provide before she ever thought to ask.

Hackles rising at the thought of tasting her delectable skin, his cock a steel band of reckless want that refused to relent—even after all these months—he shivered. After losing himself between those honeyed thighs too many times to count, abstaining from drinking her down, and resisting the rut, he still couldn't go an hour without wanting more.

He was desperate to sate her primal needs, to ease her appetite for rebellion with his knot, going to great lengths to ensure her belly never rumbled. That her thirst for what the general could pump down her throat was at her disposal, always.

Unbidden, a growl rumbled up through Giaus' diaphragm. His tongue flicking back to front, he swiped his sensory pits clear of the stink of charred smoke and spat into the embers.

For months, he'd been waiting for his eyes to tell him what the Sight already knew. So he might see the change in her slender body as she swelled with the promise of new life. For any hint that she was aware they'd been successful, that she'd been conquered. And in doing so, had tamed them all, his wildling queen who ruled them with soft coos and sharp lines.

A band of obsessive want flared behind his laces. Kicking at his leathers, where his dick grew fat and heavy with the need to fill his sensory pits with her. To taste and see and smell all that she was.

He couldn't wait.

Knew just what would happen if he let Sin at her and didn't intervene, the selfish spoiled prick.

The shift was effortless, the Sight showing him what only those in his line might see.

Slick that never went out of season, she was a beacon. Hard to follow, at first, for she'd been everywhere he looked. She'd taken to wandering the compound at night, almost unable to remain in her nest while the moons were ripe and the light was low. As if they didn't notice the flat, reflective disks glaring back at them from the shadows. That her pupils shone green in the way of a night thing.

Nocturnal.

The truth of her night vision was just another secret Giaus waited for her to divulge.

A treasure he'd wait for her to give in her own time.

If she needed patience, she would have it.

A curse echoed up from the den. Deep in the nesting pit the unlikely trio shared.

"She's gone!" Sin snarled, bolting up from the dark. Mane standing on end, fury billowed off his shoulders in waves of panic Giaus could almost taste.

The king blinked and banished the Sight. "Gone?"

"The little bitch ran." A choked bark of laughter and pain burst over the general's lips. "Gone. *Again*. I fucking knew it," he hissed, vibrating as he shoved past Giaus so he could send a frantic scowl over the Queen's Landing. "By the Nine. I fucking told you she'd run! That her domesticated act was exactly that."

The insult saw Giaus' testicles draw up, tucked flush against his body where they dumped homicidal levels of testosterone directly into his blood. "Slow down," he snapped, trying to master himself. To smother the flare of his mane and think before he struck the general down with the back of one fist. And then the other. "She's here somewhere, she couldn't have—"

A crack.

It caught his eye.

A little glimmer of temptation and darkness that shouldn't have been—and right down the middle, a twisting trail of golden damnation that led *away.*

Someone had left the gate open.

Unblinking, the king took a step he didn't bother to muffle. First one, and then three more. Faster and faster, until he was sprinting with all the grace of an earthquake.

"We have to prepare the others to hunt," Sin gasped, shivering with something beyond fury. A thing they shared.

Terror.

The queen was a vicious warrior in spirit *only.* A treasure Giaus would indulge and spoil until she hissed and demanded her space.

But she was also a slave to instinct, a babe among beasts. Kept ignorant of the dangers of life without her pack of devoted slaves. Delicate these last months, when her scent had only just begun to hint at something profound.

"Trail's going cold," Sin rasped and pushed both hands through his hair. Making fists in the bristling hair at his shoulders. And then, head tipped back, one pupil flat and black, the other reflecting a misty sheen of silver, he said, "It's been hours, Giaus. How the fuck—"

A glance passed between them. Both shaking with a possessive horror neither had known before.

That she would dare to risk her safety while in such a delicate state, to expose herself to the dangers that lay beyond the wall? At the mercy of a vicious place, teeming with predators who wouldn't hesitate to end something both males would die to defend.

Their legacy.

Season endlessly ripe, no matter that breeding her was no longer possible, hers was a scent that would draw predators and competitors alike. For hundreds of miles in every direction. Downwind, upstream... through mountains and brimstone.

She was a gift.

A Hathorian queen capable of things only the Nine might possibly know.

Filling his lungs with the dregs of her scent, Giaus shucked the mantle of leadership and became the beast.

An explosion ripped free of his chest. Echoed by his counterpart scarcely a heartbeat later, it was a challenge and a summoning in one. A notice to anything with ears or cock or half a functioning brain that she was claimed. That to touch the queen—in any way—was to evoke the primal, territorial rage that was her King and her Eye.

Completely.

Before he and Sin made a gift of their screams. Painted a beautiful mosaic of their devotion to the queen worth kneeling for.

As one, the Anhur bolted through the open gate.

Forgot to order their brethren to hunt, and vanished into the hostile night.

Ignoring the scavengers watching from the tallest branches, their pace was frantic. Their senses primed for any whisper of her passing. Any sound or muffled squeak, for after all... the dead couldn't be bothered to make such haunting music.

There was nothing but ominous silence. Shadows that would have obscured her path, were it not for the Sight that kept them on track.

"I don't understand," Sin said, lips peeled back from his teeth as he panted. Sending every desperate breath over his sensory pits. "Her trail... it... wanders. Lazy. And... confused." He shook himself hard enough to crack his neck. "You know what happens if she"— he snarled, musk billowing off his skin in heated waves, the rut flooding in to obliterate all else—"if something else gets her."

Giaus' heart lurched at the thought. Of her fine, elegant bones broken. Poking through cherished, pale skin.

And then the wind turned and showed them the stench of a nightmare trapped in moldering flesh.

A mountain moved.

Bending saplings, it lumbered through the woods, coughing up a painful sound. Its skin twisting in a nauseating fashion with every mismatched step it managed to claim.

Months of filth caked on monstrous deformities, it had been waiting long enough to blend in with its surroundings. To go unnoticed, even to them. Those who could see with uncommon eyes.

"Fuck," Sin whispered, hands falling lax at his sides as he watched the beast approach. Jaw falling open around a breathless, *"Balkazar."*

A peculiar buzzing rattled through Giaus' skull, making his mane stand on end. His shoulders were tight, newly grown claws dimpling his palms as best they could. And the sound that bubbled forth? It was an inferno. Annihilation and endless torment, a sound that made a monster cringe and moan. Piss dribbling between bowed hind legs.

Balkazar who'd dared.

Who'd touched the queen and made her cry.

Who was absolutely drenched in Renegade's scent.

And there, hanging from his lower jaws... the edge of a silky black fur cloak he'd gifted her from the finest pelt.

"I owe you a debt," Giaus snarled, and let the tempest consume his every deranged inch. "And I promise you will suffer before you die."

It was Sin who stepped between them. Who signaled for patience and snarled, "Where is she?"

For a moment, it seemed the words could not penetrate so thick and deformed a skull. That the animal's brain was little more than a hank of salt and fat, jiggling with the occasional electric frizzle.

And then, with the ominous crack of bone bending under grotesque weight, Balkazar lifted the smaller of his arms to point. Shuffling three staggering steps to the left so they could see behind his bulk.

Her trail bolted into the bush. A golden, erratic line of a female now set on evasion. Fleeing as she ought.

Relief brought an instant of clarity to the king's mind. And it took everything he had to force, "What are you doing here?" through the edge of clenched teeth.

Incomprehensible sounds burbled over the beast's hideous lips, but there was only one worth deciphering. One that sent bile splashing up to burn the back of Giaus' throat. Blood to rush and roar in his ears.

It came again. A hissing rattle in a voice mangled with a phlegmy growl.

"*Priiigusssss...*"

Sin's head tipped to one side. "I don't—"

But Giaus *did*. He knew exactly what the war chief had come to say. Understood what the Unworthy lech had managed to turn away from in his bid to die for the Karahmet bloodline, for only the king knew what commanded the Legion.

But he could only force two words through frozen vocal cords.

And they trembled with the effort.

"He's coming."

20

A shade moved through the gloom. Followed by one, then five more. Stalked by a veil of silence, for in their wake lurked the scavengers fattened by scraps. Those who knew that when the shadows took to the night, a bounty of excess was sure to follow.

At the flick of one pointed ear, the shadows spilled forth. Circling around a dense clearing dappled with the gentle white light of the triplet moons.

Highlighting the herd, the moonlight glanced off the curved edge of great, sweeping horns that shielded muscular necks. Built-in protection for deep, cavernous torsos. The grazers were tucked in tight as they slept. The razor edge of their horns made a deadly circle watched over by the young bucks.

It was a perfect defense, their instincts for survival without flaw, they'd evolved to be invulnerable to any but the very best of the apex predators ruling these woods.

A soft click of the tongue no louder than the wind breaking a twig.

The shadows tightened their noose, waiting for the signal to strike.

Bearing only backward-facing teeth lining angular muzzles, claws, and dexterous tails, they were commanded by the juggernaut queen perched on an armored shoulder. A titan who wielded the deadliest weapon the wilds had ever known...

... and the Shade who'd tamed her vicious heart.

Opportunity came on a cloud.

Hanging ripe in the night sky, dark with impending thunder, it blotted out the dappled silver light.

Sultana's crimson frill bloomed open. Silent, the color muted in the half-light, her claws dug into the gaps in the scales her mother had once worn. Alien pupils a vertical slash of spite and unflinching hunger, she made her choice. Selected her target, and opened her jaws.

Blond ears flicked back and tucked tight to his skull, her master tilted his chin in the opposite direction. Allowing her to vent the warbling tri-toned cry that incapacitated the yearling grazer marked for death.

It went to its knees with a grunt, a seizure shuddering through limbs now rigid and flailing. Convulsions rippling through tender flesh not yet toughened by seasons of hardship.

From every direction, shadows bled into the clearing. Snarling and snapping, they sent chaos through the herd.

Sending up an alarm too late, the herd bolted into the wood. Lowing and groaning as they moved to protect their young and weak. Abandoning the young buck who couldn't muster the will to fight—not with his brain jiggling inside its case and blood pouring from flared nostrils.

As one, the reptiles fell on their meal.

And by the time Sultana took her next breath, the buck was dead.

And what a horrible death it had been. Bloody. Painful. At the mercy of dragons who didn't care if their meal was wriggling or rotting.

They merely gulped, swallowed, and gulped again.

"I have to teach you some manners," their master murmured through the point of his canines. Pushing a tattooed hand through his hair as he strolled into the clearing and sent Sultana onto her kill. "Ladies first," he cooed, watching the queen fall into the spilled belly of ropey intestines, for the lava-kin preferred the ease of nutrient-dense organ meats to flesh.

At least at first.

But the wryms were growing.

Faster than he'd thought possible when

he thought of how helpless and tiny they'd been mere months prior. When he'd meant to make a meal of Sultana and her siblings... before even the *thought* of her broken and mutilated caused him grief.

Already, they weighed more than he did, despite being half his size.

Already her bulk was a burden when she demanded to perch with her claws on one side, and her tail wrapped around his narrow shoulders.

Trilling, Sultana shimmied back, shaking her head and neck. Wrenching something free with a squelch of ripping meat, she returned to stand at his side. Dropping a jiggly hunk of what looked to be liver at his feet, she sent her long, serpentine tongue over her muzzle and teeth before slurping that forked appendage back between her lips.

It flicked out again to taste the wind. His mood. Sussing out even the slightest hint of danger or opportunity. Her senses a deadly sharpened blade he trusted implicitly.

He grinned, showing the point of deadly teeth. "All for you, my lady. My larders are full, remember?" He reached and scratched beneath her pointed, angular chin. Fingers inching back to tease the edge of her frill until she sent a playful snap at his wrist. "Gotta keep you nice and fat so you and your thralls don't get any clever ideas about putting Hathorian meat on the menu."

She blinked, and in one sinuous movement, caught her unwelcome gift between her teeth, threw her head back, and swallowed. Neck sliding side to side in a bunching, serpentine curve as she forced that mouthful down into her gullet.

Movement.

Breaking branches that shattered the hush.

Hissing, his wryms fell into a possessive snarl over their kill. Warbling a deep, thrumming growl, Sultana thumped her tail on the ground. A hollow crash loud enough to be unmistakable for what it was.

A warning.

The only one she'd bother to issue.

Slipping into the dark, the Hathorian male blended into the shadows that called to him. Fingers dancing over the hilt of his obsidian blades. Clear of Sultana's path, should she need to incapacitate with her horrible song, he claimed an angle none of the wryms had covered. Strategic. Calm. His wrist cocked and ready to flick one of his many obsidian blades into the throat or eyes of whatever was stupid enough to ignore Sultana's warning.

Clicking his tongue twice, he held the wryms back until he knew just what it was that dared to interrupt their meal.

Something small shoved through the underbrush. Careless, a soft grunt of effort and a hiss that was decidedly not animal.

Fingers growing slick on his blade, his jaw flexed.

Infected.

He'd only seen a handful of loners since setting the horde on Balkazar. But every one of them demanded respect.

After all, he had no mercy for the hopeless lost.

Only vengeance.

Only hatred burned where his heart had once been soft.

Movement caught his eye, and with ears pressed flat, he sank deeper into the shadows.

Nothing at all could have prepared him for what came through the brambles.

She burst into the clearing in a shaft of moonlight. A swirl of tattered nightdress, all elegant fine bones and snarls of wild loose hair. Skin pale and unblemished.

A creature of his most cherished fantasies, in the flesh.

"Renegade," he breathed, and his heart cracked. Bleeding where it had broken, this one final time.

Of course she'd be here. Alive, in whatever capacity that word meant for her, now. She was a survivor, in any state. A true queen, no matter the corruption in her blood. All lush curves and tempting peaks.

Sighing, she lifted her arms high above her head, stretched, pulled the night deep into her lungs, and exhaled a coy smirk. "I presume you've got control of these lizards?"

Startled, he reeled back—and gave away his hiding place.

She took a step toward Sultana, palms up.

Sultana's frill snapped open, beaming deadly crimson, the not-so-tiny wrym coiled around herself and prepared to kill for a second time in the space of an hour.

"Sultana, no!" he shouted because he couldn't help himself.

It was Renegade.

She turned to face him, then. An eerie smooth action that did not falter or hitch, she found where he lurked without any whisper of effort.

Gold.

Ringing pupils blown so wide, he could see the reflection of the moons shimmering in those pools of inky black.

Infected.

Lost. Beyond all hope of rescue.

There was no denying it now. No chance that she'd miraculously managed to escape unscathed, she belonged to Giaus.

Utterly.

"Sickle," she purred, and the sound made his breath stutter in his chest.

"Not another step," he hissed, slipping through the shadows until he stood at Sultana's side. Half a pace behind her deadly muzzle. Exposed, yes. But there was no safer place in all the wilds, than behind that shimmering crimson frill. "Stay exactly where you are, or I'll loose Sultana."

Ears pricked forward, Renegade chuckled and flashed her palms. "Incredible," she whispered and did not blink. Not even once. Entirely too still as she licked her lips and stared. "You've trained them?"

It wasn't that simple, not by a long shot. But to explain that the neonates had imprinted on him—in part due to his armor made of their mother's impenetrable hide, her stink glands, and teeth—and he'd spent these last months learning to utilize the unique talents of the most deadly predator ever known was far more complicated than the simple, "Yes," that spilled over his lips.

"Incredible," she said again, head tilting to the side. "I thought you were dead. We *all* thought you were dead. Sickle—"

"*That's not my name*," he spat. Lips peeling back to expose his canines.

She paused. Blinked. "We thought you were dead. When I caught your scent"—she shook her head—"I thought I'd find something much different than... *Look at you.*" She took a half-step before she remembered the warning. "You look... incredible. Is that armor made of dragon scales?"

"I'm sorry," he whispered and choked back the salty burn of tears. "It was all my fault. What happened to you. That I was too fucking weak to save you from"—he pulled a breath through his teeth and scrubbed at inked cheeks—"*him*. He ruined you, and I'm sorry, but I can give you peace. It won't hurt, I promise."

A dainty trill left her lips, and she laughed. The sound sending a thousand little barbs into his wretched heart. "Ah, yes," she cooed, eyes flashing an eerie green in the silver light. "Fuck the Anhur. Greedy selfish cunts. Killing me would certainly learn them a lesson, but..." She flicked a smile at him, meeting his teary gaze with something fierce and wild. "If you can be tempted to wait... I have so much to tell you..."

Swallowing, the Omega male couldn't help the easy slide of his eyes. Watching as she stole another step closer. "Renegade," he hissed and put a restraining hand on Sultana's frill.

"We're nocturnal," she murmured and tore her eyes away from his to gaze into the night. "Did you know that?"

"Why are you here, Renegade?"

Instead of answering, her smile grew sad. "I didn't. Didn't even know the word 'nocturnal' until I heard them use it. They keep us ignorant by design. Isolated in the dark. Servants to suit their every need. Bred from the back," she hissed, and her ears flicked back. Flattened. "Ignorant," she said again. "Because knowledge is power, and they want us dependent."

Moving with careful stolen millimeters, he pulled one of the long blades from its sheath where it was hidden at his lower back.

"I don't blame him for it, not really," she drawled, and her head ticked off to the right. Attention caught by the fluttering wings of a moth. "Sin was doing as he was trained. Keeping secrets like treasures is their nature —*please don't do that.*"

He froze.

A drop of sweat rolled down his back, beneath the armor he'd fashioned for himself and never took off.

She flashed her palms. "Please. I don't have a lot of time, and there's so much you don't know." She smiled again, and it was... horrible and beautiful, all at once. Gleaming gold and feral. "About our culture. What we're capable of, in the dark. The threat we pose to a predatory species who could easily tear us in half but won't. *Can't.*"

He couldn't help the intrigue—but he wasn't foolish enough to relinquish his blades. "I'm listening."

"We can choose," she whispered. "Hathorian females. It's our choice, to breed or not. To reject what they pump inside."

"That..." He shook his head. "I had no idea," he returned, mindlessly stroking Sultana's brow ridge as the others fell back into their meal.

"Neither did I," she murmured, and her eyes flashed green as she glanced at him through the gloom.

He understood it, of course. Why the Anhur needed to keep a secret like that. It could unsettle the entire Silver Court. Whole harems might be culled if the Omegas refused to breed for the Anhur.

It was the sort of whisper that could get a generation of Hathorians obliterated, not that learning it now was any sort of dangerous out here.

But something else she said caught his attention. "Why are you short on time?"

At this, she glared into the wood. Back, to where she'd come. "They aren't thrilled about my wandering the night."

And because he couldn't help himself, because he needed to hear her say it, he said, "They?"

For a moment, Renegade's eyes drifted away as she looked where he couldn't see. Inside. Strumming the bond she shared with a beast.

And then, "Furious doesn't begin to describe what Giaus is right now," she murmured, and a sick little smile bent the edge of her lips. "And Sin... he's—"

Knuckles going white, he blurted, *"Sinadim is alive?"*

She paused, head drifting off to the side as she peered at him through the dark. One ear tipped forward, the other back.

And then, very carefully, "Sinadim is dead in much the same way I suspect Sickle died."

He swallowed, *hard.*

"But I'm still Renegade." She chirped then shrugged. "Just... better."

"They're coming. For you," he said, and it wasn't a question. Lower back bunching as he cast a nervous glance into the gloom, he clicked his tongue and sent Sultana into the wood.

Warbling, irritated to be drawn away from a fresh kill, she went and took her thralls with her. There one second, gone the next. Lurking in the gloom as they guarded the clearing.

Only then did he ask, "Renegade, *why did you come here?*"

She took a step, the golden rim of her eyes catching the moonlight and throwing it back in his face. "Yarrow root grows where the soil is acidic," she whispered. "In the dark. Under the loam. Where no light shines, except that from an evenwood."

Nausea bubbled up. Sour and hot, it seared the back of his throat. And for the first time, he retreated half a pace, already sick with jealousy, no matter that he knew she was untouchable. Eyes traveling over her slender frame, he saw what was swollen and ripe. "You're pregnant."

"I was banished from the Silver City," she said, switching tracks without a blink. "Not executed. Banished. My... *mother...* she would brew me a foul, bitter tea every time I returned from Hadim's rooms. When my season struck and there was no more anonymity in the dark. With one hand,

Samina tore out her throat, and so the last thing she said was a lie."

A cloud crossed over the brightest moon, plunging Renegade into shadows. "I-I'm sorry," he said, swallowing back the shiver. "I knew Samina well. Better than most, probably. That must have been... I'm sorry."

And then in a husky, desperate voice he did not recognize, she said, "*The girl had no part in—*"

Renegade choked. Pale white fingers found her windpipe, clutching, as if to keep herself whole. Lost in the past, where he couldn't touch her. "They banished me when what I really earned," she said, pacing ever closer, "was an execution."

"You knew what the tea was," he guessed because there could be no other answer to a question as old as this one.

The smile slipped off her lips, and her fingers fell to the cradle below her belly button. Where she was ripe. "I regret only that I lied to save myself. That I allowed my fear of Hadim to tarnish her memory for *nothing*. He docked my tail anyway. It made him hard to give it back to me. A twitching gift that died in my hands."

At this, he sighed. Listening to her macabre confession, despite the urge to flee from this slender fledgling predator stalking him through the night. Circling with careful, deliberate intention.

"I came because the Anhur lied to me,"

Renegade hissed. "My mates. Sin, who used his knowledge against me. And Giaus, who kept the secret and benefited most. *They made a transaction of me*," she snarled, ears flat, eyes gleaming pools of vibrant green. "Because they cannot help themselves. They're animals," she spat. "And I came to teach them what pain is. How deadly hope can be when it is given only to be ripped away."

The wind whistled through the trees, banishing the cloud cover blocking out the moons.

And when he could see her beloved face once more...

... it was wet with tears.

"I came because I thought I couldn't live another day in that den. Reduced to nothing more than a pampered doll who never wants for food or comfort. My every need attended before I even think it."

"But you want more," he said, knowing it to be true, having drunk deeply of her brand of freedom for himself.

"There was something *missing*," she said, correcting him. Her hips rolling as she paced around him. Clinging to shadows and swells in a way that held him enthralled to her every circling step.

"Renegade," he warned and matched her step for step. Mindful of the slippery broken corpse still steaming in the grass. The wicked edge of curved horns only half as cutting as the look gleaming in her alien eyes.

"I have a king," she murmured and sank into a crouch. "The queen's Authority, the one who wears my crown."

Armor sliding without so much as an errant whisper, he mirrored her posture, planting both fists into the loam—and his knuckles sank into a pool of cooling gore.

"I named my general." Her ears flicked back, but she grinned, watching from beneath her lashes. "The queen's Eye, who sees where the path leads."

"And now you want a Shade?" he drawled and brought his feet beneath him. "The queen's Shadow, who guards her back with a thunder of dragons."

Gleaming eyes flashed green in the dark. "Ahh," she breathed, and it was as if she'd been given a gift. "I thought I came for vengeance," she said. "But instead I found *you*. Thriving in the wild beyond, in spite of the Anhur. And I now I know."

He hummed, but that was all.

"Without a queen, they're nothing at all. But a queen without a shadow cannot rule the feral court, because she's already dead." She flicked a quick lethal smile at him. "I mean to claim what I am owed, and I came bearing gifts."

She lunged.

21

She was on him before he could dart clear of her toxic touch. Landing a playful blow that glanced off his armored shoulder, she bounded away and rolled into shadows, where she knew his eyes could not follow.

Not yet.

"Renegade," he spat, ears flicked back, he flashed the point of his teeth—but only tucked in deeper. Dug in, he tried to track her with the slide of those honeyed eyes that could not truly see.

"Shade," she hummed, ignoring the warning. Rolling his chosen name around in her mouth, just because she liked the taste.

He turned, keeping any weak spots tucked away. "I will not join you."

"You reject what you do not understand." Lunging, she struck anew, sending a bare foot lashing out at his ankle.

He caught her calf and tossed it away with

246

a laugh. Cold, a bark of derision and hurt. "I reject a new queen! One infected by Anhur greed, playing games *she does not understand*. How long?" he snarled, and shucked his bracers so she could see the swirling beauty of inked skin. "How long before you decide you can make me prettier? Before you tire of me, and trade my skills for a new set that suit your flighty moods?"

It was her turn to listen, and she did so without a blink or breath. Stalling their games, so he might vent this anguish for the wrongs done to him. To their people.

Wrongs that would never be allowed to happen again.

"I will not kneel, Renegade," he said, voice trembling. "Not to you. Not ever again." Tattooed cheeks flushing with glowing heat that made her itch to touch, he sneered.

Thumbing the tie that bound her cloak, she stood, straightening. "It can't be coincidence," she breathed, and slid her feet through the spongy loam of dewy grass. "Both of us here. Blooming in the dark we were born to rule."

He scoffed. "Balkazar said much the same thing—right before he promised to breed me to one of our daughters. Is that why you're here?" A scowl marred his beauty. Wild. Eyes rimmed in the brilliant, white-hot of seething hatred. A loathing, she knew, on some level, she had not earned. "Running errands for your masters?"

A snarl spattered over her lips. "Balkazar is *not* my creation."

Shade exhaled a shuddering breath, his temper already cooling where vile words still hung in the air. "Is he dead, then?"

Clearing her throat, she inspected her cuticles for a beat, then said, "There aren't words to describe what Balkazar has become," before she turned. Pulling the ties and loosening her nightdress.

"Good." Shade relented, pushing both hands through his hair, tugging on the blond velvet of twitching ears. "*Good.* A fitting end for that festering sack of sewage."

Lifting one shoulder, Renegade shrugged. Content, for a moment, to let the stillness of the night carry away all that was toxic and cruel, for it was a thing she was deeply intimate with. The sludge of anger and fear that trauma left in its wake.

And then, "They're smothering me. It doesn't matter how hard they try, how deep their concern. They cannot feel... *me.* What they're doing to me."

"*You* claimed *them,*" he reminded her.

As if she could ever forget. "It was a gift they both welcomed."

"That's what it is to be Hathorian," he said, and she saw the suffering that sparkled on his lashes. "To give and expect nothing in return."

She took a step, toying with the weight of her shirt and her words in equal measure.

"We're on the edge of something new. Out here, in a place where we all might start fresh. Names chosen for our deeds, not our coveted bloodlines. Where we can choose who rules the court and build something to be proud of." Another careful step, this one squishing between her toes. Tacky with crimson that shimmered and tossed sparkling light into her sensitive eyes. "Maybe it was the Nine. Or fate. But it's happening with or without you, Shade."

"Renegade"—he scoffed—"you're infected! You cannot ask this of me."

Tongue darting out, she tipped her face back. Soaking in the moonlight. "I'm asking for your help. Your guidance. That you stand at my side and grant me the wisdom you earned in the court of our enemies. And yes," she whispered, showing him the blunted edge of her teeth. Close enough to reach out and press one dainty palm to his armored chest. "I'm asking for your fealty. That you kneel, but only to me, and in return?" She retreated with a playful shove. "You get the night."

Honeyed eyes grew slitted, his ears tipped forward. Head tilted.

"You think it a coincidence?" she said again and turned. Letting the edge of her nightdress droop, the moonlight playing off her shoulder... a spot she knew he lusted after, as any Hathorian male might. "That you hunt at night? Even the name you've chosen is a tribute to this new kingdom blooming under the stars, *Shade*."

She bolted, knowing he would follow. That he couldn't help but chase the lure she'd set.

"I will give it to you," she called and slipped between the saplings. Her path an easy one to pace, where it hummed through her mind. A destination she alone could see, for to her, it was a beacon. One that called her home. "I will give you gifts no Anhur can ever know. Secrets written in a language only we can read."

"Renegade," he gasped and shoved through a bramble to stand at her side. "What—"

He sucked a breath between the points of his canines.

Exhaled wonder that lit his tattooed face from within.

An eerie green glow lit an intimate clearing. That of a fully mature evenwood blooming at night. In its many branches, lunar moths fluttered and danced, taking tiny sips from flower cups. Sweet nectar raining down in drips and drops. At her feet, dozens of fungi throwing spores. Moss and clover a carpet that carried the delicate scent of earth and sweet herbs.

"This," she whispered and slipped around the trunk. Coy. Leading, her hand trailing on the smooth bark that seemed to shiver at her touch. "It is ours. And when you can see what I see…"

With stars in her eyes, she slapped the lowest hanging branch—and sent the night things to the wind.

A thousand glittering wings took flight, and even to Shade's weak eyes, they sparkled. Showering them in dust. In magic one might only find in the arms of the night.

"Join me," the queen murmured and pressed her forehead to the trunk. "Take your place at my side. My guiding shadow. Be my balance in a court already too heavy with Anhur influence and through you…" She smiled, showing blunted teeth. "A generation of not-quite Hathorians who can be proud of their legacy. Who will know where they come from, taught by one who knows their history. Who *lived* it."

For a moment, as he watched the moths dancing on the wind, there was nothing. Only the faint hum of music that promised… *more.*

And then, "Take it off," he snarled, deft, inked fingers working to shuck his armor.

Grinning, she obeyed with a flick of her wrist, for she'd already half-done the job. Mouth watering as she waited for her prize to be revealed because she knew they fit.

Her breath hitched as she watched him peel off the armored plates. The wind teased the tips of peaked nipples, making her cold where she was desperately wet.

Still, as she waited. Ready, for she had three things yet to give him.

When he stood before her in all his, naked, inked glory...

... she dropped to her knees. Wrists on her thighs. Eyes downcast.

And gave her submission. Kneeling for the last member of her court. Swollen with the get of the other two.

Not as a slave, but a queen who freely gave what she had left to share with a male she'd chosen entirely herself. One she'd hunted and tracked because she knew he'd been made for her. That *he* was the missing piece who could make her whole.

A strangled sound died in his throat, and he reached with trembling fingers. His touch landed on her chin. Tilting her head back as he gazed into her eyes with those that were liquid sugar.

Without a blink, she let her lips fall apart. Left her mouth open as her tongue peeked over her bottom teeth. Enticing. Lewd. *Victorious.*

In an instant, he broke. Feeding her everything he had in a single, careful thrust, he let her taste. Gentle, despite the way he shook.

She let him take, knowing he'd never been allowed to do so before.

Only reaching up to cup his swollen sack. To invite him deeper. Enjoying the weight, the way his balls flexed and bunched, held tight to his body.

At her touch, ecstasy burst on her tongue. Pushed into the sensory pits lining the roof of her mouth, she fell into the closest thing to the rut she'd ever know. One brought on *without* the influence of the Anhur.

This was the flavor of a male she'd make her own.

One who matched.

"I know you can feel them," he gasped and wrapped tattooed fingers around the bulge of his modest knot where it had begun to swell at his base. Pulling back, so he could trace her lips with little beads of salted want. "How long do we have?"

She sucked him between her lips. Nursing at his engorged tip that shone tight and painful beneath the glow of the Evenwood. And when she released him with a pop, it was to shrug and say, "As long as it takes."

Forearm braced against the trunk of the Evenwood, he looked down. Pain and wonder etched into his brow.

She'd chosen well for her last.

Shade was beautiful and fierce. A true survivor who'd done things she'd never thought possible. Things Giaus himself would have to commend when he saw what the smallest of them had accomplished.

Her Omega male.

"Renegade," he whispered, and his fingers grew tight in her hair. Making snarls in the fine black silk Giaus so loved to pet. "I'm—"

Swallowing around his end, she took him

to the root and sent a single, damning purr straight through to his balls. Meaning to drink him down. To know the taste of him this way, before she had him everywhere else.

Inside and out.

It didn't take long.

With a strangled grunt, those honeyed eyes were hidden beneath a furrowed brow. Shuddering, he sent jet after jet of pent-up seed to paint the back of her tongue.

Still, she purred. Singing an altogether new song for the male more precious than any living in the beyond.

He hissed, one hand buried in her hair, and hauled her up. Cock still kicking where it pressed hot and insistent against the gentle swell of her belly. Where new life grew ripe and healthy.

"Lift your leg," he barked, and his free hand slid down. Over the curve of her hip...

... and his fingers traced the hard ridge of her second gift.

She felt it when he realized. When the breath was torn from his lungs in a rush that wheezed his shock. "Your tail. It's—"

"A secret between only us," Renegade whispered and nosed the junction between jaw and shoulder. Letting her tongue trail along the wiry muscle stained with the ink of his former queens. Lips catching on the place where she ached to set her own mark, the kind that went so much deeper than mere ink and pain. "A gift for the future, if you'll take it."

A sob stuttered between clenched teeth, but that was all before he was on her. Lips, tongue, teeth, Shade took what was offered. Hiking her thigh up and over his hip, he swiped his cock through sodden folds and plunged inside. Knot teasing her rim, he fucked her with every ounce of unspoken feeling he possessed.

And never once did he blink. Not a moment was lost or missed.

Not when he cupped the swell of one ripe breast, rolling her nipple between forefinger and thumb. Not when she arched her back and urged him on, riding him where he held her pinned in place, soaking him in slick that ran out of season.

"Please," she whispered, ears laid out. Begging for permission, so she could give what she'd come to claim.

He lunged.

Lips crashing into hers, he kissed her. Deeply, his breath spilling into her as his knot bloomed, stretching where she was tight.

And it was enough.

He was enough.

Eyes rolling back, she came. Milking his knot as he offered pleasure. Her chin tipped back, to expose that stretch of pale skin never blemished before.

With a snarl, he broke from her lips and

set his teeth. Marking his queen, Shade bred a female who belonged to a prince who'd died to save him. A queen owned by the king who'd taken everything Shade might have loved.

A female who belonged to him now, too.

A new claim shoved aside the other two, and Renegade whined as she was marked. Exquisite anguish bled through him into her, a cooling wave that brought sanity and salvation, for in an instant that rippled through her soul, all her scattered pieces were knit back together. Made whole.

Teeth locked in place, he shuddered into his queen. Sending jet after jet of seed spilled too late to claim the life ripening in her womb, he pumped her full and sealed her tight.

She sobbed, for with a lovely coo, he took half her burden into his own heart. Tattooed fingers slipped up, over the nub of her budding tail. Tracing her spine, her shoulders, the back of her neck, and into her hair, he guided her lips to the spot left clear of ink.

Where she'd always meant to put her mark.

"I claim you, Shade of the Feral Court," she said, lips moving against the warmth of his skin. Drowsy and languid in the aftermath of so violent and tender a breeding. And then, simply, "Mine, bound until death."

And then she gave him the night.

22

Clenching his fist just to feel his claws extend, Sin scowled. Furious and impressed all at once, for the clever, glorious little bitch was using the Sight against them.

They'd tracked her deep into the wood to a clearing darkened by a dense canopy high above. One with the grass cropped short by dozens of grazers, piles of dung... and a corpse that hadn't been picked clean.

The meat, still mostly intact, was turning rancid in the muggy heat, despite the rain threatening to burst from dark clouds.

It wasn't a good omen.

"No scavengers?" Sin murmured, his every available sense primed to defend or attack.

To this, Giaus' only response was a brief flare of his mane. An acknowledgment that didn't distract, for the king was fixated on the puzzle before him, still sifting through the scents littering the clearing.

And it *was* a puzzle.

All through the clearing and the trees, Renegade had left spinning trails of gold that shimmered on the wind. Running circles, leaving golden fingerprints of her delectable scent scattered through the wood, she'd all but obliterated their Sight. Overwhelming them with a trail they couldn't help but follow—even if it led in hopeless circles.

Because she was toying with them. Playing games, when she should be back in their den. Hidden away from the truth Giaus had only just revealed.

Jaw flexing, Sin worked to contain his temper. Banished the Sight, and left the king to it. Knowing the other to be more experienced in enduring these wilds, that between them, Giaus was the better tracker.

Sin's talents lay elsewhere. In strategic planning. For war—or the capture of one wayward, infuriating mate who didn't know the truth.

She'd run an incredible distance from the Queen's Landing, given her tiny stature and extra precious burden she carried. It spoke of just how significant her head start had been. Proportional to how much energy he and Giaus had spent to run her down, sprinting through what remained of the night and into the morning.

It was an advantage she'd taken full advantage of, despite the risk or the consequences. That she'd had some kind of interaction with Balkazar, *survived*, and then continued on her merry fucking way?

"I'm thinking chains," Sin hissed, and kicked the corpse that still had give. Not yet in rigor mortis, the joints still mobile enough to flop when he nudged it with the edge of his boot. "Thick ones. Really, *really* heavy with a leash no longer than the length of the nest. See if she runs again."

But then, the blame wasn't entirely on her narrow shoulders, was it? She'd survived the wilds before. Evaded pack and horde and predators alike for longer than should have been possible for a mere harem slave.

No, the fault was shared with the king. Giaus, who'd known what horrors thrived in the wilds and had kept his secrets.

Mane bristling, Sin shivered and shot a vicious glare at the king. Irate, for Giaus had only revealed the bitter truth of their bloodline because Balkazar—of all the vile creatures—had forced it out of him.

Only then, did he name what lurked out in the wild.

A demon, apparently. One even the Nine had cause to fear.

The *Primus.*

What had once been some nameless Anhur from ancient times long past, now sat in the heart of the horde. It was the brain of the Legion. The bottomless stomach. Ageless, a colossus had grown impossibly large through countless seasons of vicious cannibalism.

"Why?" Sin snarled for the fourth time, relentless in his irritation. Badgering the king until he got an answer that wasn't a surly grunt. "*Why* wouldn't you tell us? Giaus—we could have prepared!"

At this, the king roared and whirled with claws and bristling mane, reeking of musk that warned of his temper. "There is no preparation that will stop the Primus!" His pupils tiny pricks of terrified rage he'd only dared to show Sin, he huffed out a pale attempt at a laugh. "No fortification strong enough. No wall the Legion can't scale with sheer numbers. All we can do is build a den and keep her locked away, hidden from the wind, because if the Primus catches her scent... if he even suspects a creature like her exists? The Legion will march on the Queen's Landing before we have the chance to build an army. Before any of you are strong enough to do more than die honorably. An endless line of infected more gruesome than you can possibly imagine will march through that wall. Over their dead. Obliterating any pitiful defense we can possibly erect. They will not stop, Sin. If it takes years and more bodies than exist in the Silver City, they will never stop coming."

Thunder rolled overhead. Brought by

heavy dark clouds that obscured the glaring heat of the noon sun.

Breath that had been frozen in his chest thawed at that sound as if given permission. Releasing a slow exhale, Sin blinked. Nodded. Mind racing to find a solution. A strategy. *Anything* to refute the king's words, to see the way through, as his queen had commanded him to do.

"Okay," he said. "Then we—"

"Quiet." Giaus snapped his fingers, going still in a way that sent ice spiking through Sin's nape. His mane standing on end. "This is a trap."

From the far side of the clearing, a soft click whispered through the trees.

And the shadows came alive.

Glaring.

Five pairs of eyes watched from the dark.

They were surrounded.

"Shit," Sin spat, and pressed his right side to Giaus' left. Silently demanding the king guard his blind side, for there was no denying the nature of the beasts who hunted them with unblinking alien stares.

Predators.

Filtering the wind through his teeth, Giaus didn't respond until a thrumming, dual-toned growl spattered through the dark. Until the living shadows tightened their perimeter.

"*Fuck*," the king snarled. "Lava-kin. A yearling matriarch and her thralls."

Under his breath, the general asked, "How do you know?" without daring to tear his eye from the impromptu battlefield.

"Young matriarchs don't have lava until they lay their first clutch," he murmured, terse. Brisk. "Instead, they scream."

"Well that doesn't sound—"

"It's worse." Giaus snarled. "It's much worse."

It was Sin's turn to choke on his words, and in so doing, bloodied his palms with the points of his claws. Renegade had been *all over* this clearing. He could see her tracks as if she'd only just laid them. The foolish creature must have stumbled onto a fresh kill and—

"I'm going to need you to be a target," Giaus said. Voice low and tight with urgency, sinking to his haunches in a bid to appear smaller than the general. Less than. "When the matriarch reveals herself, make sure she sees *you*. Look for red and do whatever you can to keep her distracted. It's going to hurt," he added, and Sin could feel the challenging smirk. "A lot."

"As my fucking king commands," he drawled and cracked his neck. Shaking out his hands, claws extending and retracting as he tested their sheaths and prepared for bloodshed.

Giaus flicked a sly grin at him. "Might shit your pants."

"Try not to sound too excited," Sin returned. "Know how much you love butt stuff, my Liege."

The king chuffed, a laugh clipped short as it burst over his lips and eased the tension winding them too tight. Pushed too close to brittle. And then, "Ready?"

Sin gave a tight nod...

... and was met with applause.

Clapping followed by the high-pitched coo of amused laughter.

"*Very* clever, my king," she sang and strolled into the clearing. "But to sacrifice your general so early? Seems a touch rash. Should have brought the rest of your men."

Mouths agape, the Anhur stared at the creature who stepped into the clearing, for this was not the female they'd kept pampered and tame.

This was a warrior queen from ancient times.

Dressed from nape to ankles in fitted armor. Dark scales that blended with the dappled light of the high foliage, she stepped into their presence as if from the pages of long-forgotten myth. Hair wild and thick, shining with health where it fluttered about her shoulders. Untamed. The enticing swell of her belly was denied to their eyes, yet she appeared undamaged. Absolutely breathtaking in all her Hathorian glory.

"*Renegade*," Sin breathed, shocked stupid. His lips parting around a soundless accusation that only brought a devious smirk to her infuriating, exotic features.

She strolled between two sets of gleaming eyes, careless of the risk. "Sin. Giaus. Enjoying your outing? Nice day for a hunt, isn't it?"

The first drops of rain spattered through the leaves.

Giaus' mane rose up on a snarl, one dredged up from the bottom of his lungs. A savage thing meant to vent his temper and command his queen to obey.

Renegade's smirk only grew. Bold as she approached—and at her back, two soft clicks, another of those warbling dual-toned cries, and lava-kin bled into the clearing. Five of them from all sides. Even coiled, they stood tall enough to reach Renegade's throat.

But they didn't so much as glance as the soft thing that would make easy prey.

And still, Sin couldn't force a single word through his lips. Not a curse or a prayer. Nothing that wasn't a thin hiss of shocked breath.

He could only watch.

Horrified and aroused in equal measure.

Shivering and coiled, the wryms matched her step for step. Slitted glares fixed to Giaus where he crouched in the grass.

"I told you once," she said, painting Giaus with a slow once over, "that I would find a way to break this infernal bond."

The king let go a careful breath, and said, "You did."

For a moment, as she continued her torturous approach, she let the threat shimmer in the air. Flanked by dragons who did not blink, whose every careful step was silent in the way of something deadly looking for a meal.

"You told me," she said, and her eyes flashed green in the way of a night thing, "that I should run as fast and as far as I could because the next hunt would not be so gentle."

Giaus' tail flicked, just the once, and he sent a terse, "I did," through his teeth.

She stopped just out of reach. Just far enough away that Giaus would have to close the distance and risk engaging the wryms before the matriarch revealed herself. That he'd have to risk *her*. Renegade.

Sin glanced at his queen. Seeing what she really was, beneath it all.

Cunning.

Brilliant.

Gorgeous.

And then, through a beaming smile that split her face and challenged the sun and the triplet moons all at once, she said, "Bet you weren't expecting dragons, huh?"

Sin couldn't help the bark of laughter that escaped him, then. Incredulous, teetering on the edge of madness, he laughed.

"I trust I've made my point?" she drawled,

head tilting to the side. Ears tipped forward, her words held no heat despite the show of baffling force. "Keeping secrets is deadly business. And from this moment forward, there shall be consequences. Am I understood?"

Head thrown back, barking laughter rumbled up from deep inside Giaus' chest. "My vicious, warrior queen," he said, amber eyes positively gleaming as he looked and drank his fill. Mane shivering, one fist planted between spread knees, he balanced on his haunches. "She commands dragons!"

"Actually," she cooed, glowing from the inside out, "I don't. But *he* does."

A ghost emerged from the gloom. Dressed in a matching set of armor, tattooed brow knit with a scowl...

... hidden in the shadow of a crimson-frilled matriarch.

"May I introduce the last member of the feral court," Renegade said, the edges of a drugging purr spattering over her lips. "A beginning inside and ending. Claimed, mated. *Mine.*"

Shocked into action, Sin staggered forward. "Sic—"

"*Shade*," Renegade said, correcting him. "My Shadow, who guards my back with a thunder of dragons."

"This boy?" Giaus barked. Derisive, but not entirely cruel so much as he was shocked.

But to this, Sin could only laugh. Stepping forward with all the caution deserving of the lava-kin and the Omega who'd tamed them. Respect earned by a smaller species that had been bred to endure. "He's older than you," Sin drawled, and when Shade's ears pricked forward, the general clapped him on the shoulder. "Glad you're not dead, brother."

Shade offered a cautious smile, showing teeth when he batted Sin's hand away, and said, "Quit your mothering. I'm fine. "

Purring a seductive song, Renegade yawned. Stretched. Her ears drooping, she allowed the king to scoop her up and press her close. "Let's be going, shall we? I hear there are monsters lurking in these woods..."

23

Shifting to ease the ache bunched between her shoulders, Renegade sighed. Stretching muscles strained by the indulgence of every lewd act she could imagine—and then some.

She stood. Untangling herself from the males of her court. Sin, who watched her with hooded gaze, fist tracing the length of his rigid prick still coated in a creamy sheen.

And Shade, whose cheeks were warm and pink beneath the tattoos. Eyes glassy with all the sordid, delicious things she'd done to him, and the onset of the killing fever that brought with it great, fundamental change.

Both of them were sprawled in her nest. Contented. Fucked placid. Illuminated in the soft green light of an Evenwood tree, whose light was kind to nocturnal eyes.

At the show of her slightest interest, Giaus had uprooted it. Careful not to kill it, he'd dragged it all the way back to her den. The feat effortless for the king, but the reward for doing so?

It made their bond hum with bliss. A simple, thoughtful gift meant to feed her spirit.

She met the mutant king at the mouth of their den. One dainty hand finding the small of his back, above twitching tail she no longer had cause to be jealous of.

Because her own was growing back. Made whole by her males, who'd each given her a treasure.

"War is coming," she said. Serene as she watched the night swallow the last of the sun's heat.

Giaus hummed, bathing her in the adoration of that ravenous amber gaze. "Yes."

Below them, Sultana snapped at one of her thralls. Crimson frill flaring as she coiled and hissed.

Uttering a deep gravely chuckle, Giaus wrapped her in a fur cloak, tucking her snug beneath the weight of arms meant for murder and protection in equal measure. Filling her with all he couldn't say. And then, "Dragons may just tip the scales, but... We aren't ready."

"No," she said and sighed. Luxuriating, for a moment, in the heat of his embrace. Indulging in the male who'd given her the courage to rise and claim the dark.

As if summoned, the others joined them. Royalty and slave alike, both of them naked. All of them hers.

Deadly and strong.

Wicked and smart.

Sweet and cutting.

They were all of them a match to her rebellious fire. Obvious. Natural. Made for her, and given by the Nine.

"I don't know how long we have," she murmured, and her words held weight she was unaccustomed to wielding. "If it's months... or *years*. I don't know if we can prepare before the Legion strikes, or if we'll be swallowed whole. But war is coming to test this feral court." She smiled as she looked upon the Queen's Landing. A place that had seen bloodshed and lust. A place where dragons roosted and queens were made. "Together, we might just stand a chance."

Her hand dropped to the swell between her hips. The cradle where life had rooted. Welcome. Exciting for the promise of something profound. A thing not done before.

Giaus' palm covered hers. The king purring with deep, satisfied contentment that masked barely contained madness. Seething, primordial rage that he would gladly unleash on a whim with a song of joy and destruction in his heart. To defend what he had claimed as only he might.

"In a few short weeks," she said and felt a tiny kick against her palm. First one, then several more. "We will know if I carry a legacy or an ending. If some distant, future civilization will tell the story of the Renegade Queen and her Feral Court." She shrugged, ears flicking back as her grin grew feral. Devious. "Or we'll all be dead, and then, what does it really matter?"

"Poetic," Sin drawled and rolled his eyes.

She looked upon her general and licked her lips. Appetite building already, no matter how many times she'd had him. How often she'd tasted and touched. "First," she said, "we obliterate the horde. The Primus. Claim the wilds and rule over the secrets of a new race blessed by the Nine. Clean up the mess of weak fools who throw precious things over the wall and take no responsibility for their crimes." She paused, eyes taking him in. The scars that matched, everything else that didn't. Taken, for a moment, by the gleam of skin bronzed by the kiss of the sun.

"Giaus promised me a gargoyle," she murmured and set her cheek to her king's heat, "so I might vent my rage. Shade has given me peace, and history to shape the future. Do you recall what you promised me, Sin?"

His jaw flexed. Mismatched eyes flicking away as their bond filled with dread. Confusion and something that might have been guilt, for he'd promised her a great many things and almost all of them had been dreadful.

"I asked you once," she said, "to trade with me. That I would see Giaus fight for you against the Silver City, and in exchange—"

"Freedom," he said, the green of his eye

slid back to find her face. Cautious, he awaited her point.

"A new deal, then, to celebrate this feral court." Renegade took a step as she surveyed the fledgling kingdom rising in the wild. One with new rules and unknown limits. Poised on the edge of war. "When we march on the Silver City," she said, "you do so at my command. And when you move on the Sultan and his Heir, you do *nothing* at all until I am there to watch the disks in Hadim's spine crumble beneath your claws. From you, I shall have vengeance."

Sin watched her for the space of three breaths. Heart pounding hard enough that she could feel it clatter from his chest into hers.

And then, "Laying his head at your feet will be the most satisfying moment of my life." He knelt, grinning. Mane billowing in the evening breeze. "It shall be done, my queen."

Renegade shivered in the wind, roused by the call of the night where she ruled with velvet and fire. Serenaded by the night things, flanked by dragons, she was a conqueror that bound them. Taking nothing less than what she deserved in claiming her harem of miscreants and criminals. Those wild few who fed her spirit, satisfied her hunger, and gave her... life.

This was something new.

A place meant for the savage, where fools

could not be suffered, lest they contend with dragons and monsters. A place where they'd all been reborn, where they were happy, for now.

"This is the feral court," she whispered and her smile was deadly. Beautiful. *Free.* "And here, all must bow to the queen..."

Thank you for reading the Feral Court. Renegade and her harem will return, one day, to fight their Feral Wars... But for now, I am going to collapse into a puddle of very tired author with a new baby... and... sleep. Until then, click this link to see an INCREDIBLE NSFW version of this one-of-a-kind Zakuga cover. Trust me, you do not want to miss it. :P

If you like *free things, sneak peeks, giveaways, and super secret news about future projects*, then boiii is there a place for you! Tis called The Daniverse, and you can join by clicking the link or searching for "The Daniverse, by Myra Danvers" on Facebook.

SWALLOWED BY DARKNESS

FREE BOOK!
Download Swallowed by Darkness now!

"Thrilling, addictive, a bit horrible, but oh so entertaining and funny—truly unique—I loved it!" ~Goodreads reviewer

Cold.

The sort of cold that lined the kidneys and chilled the blood, seizing her every muscle with violent, spine-bending shivers. Nothing else was relevant. Not how she'd come to be there or why she couldn't remember... *anything.* Not her name, how old she was, or how long she'd been wherever *here* was. But it didn't matter, for she knew—without opening her eyes—this was the sort of cold no human being could withstand for long.

Groaning, she tried to pull aching limbs into the fetal position. Tried to preserve body heat and keep her vital organs warm for just a little longer, but was stopped before she'd even begun.

Bound at wrists and ankles. Legs spread wide. Hands useless at her sides.

No leverage.

Pinned. Exposed.

Panic knotted her intestines into garish ribbons, but it was too cold to scream. Too hard to open her eyes and assess her surroundings. Instead, she flexed fingers and toes, counting them. Trying to force the feeling into stiff digits. Searching for a reason that she'd be strapped to what felt like a gurney, bared and alone, with nothing between naked flesh and frigid steel. Left helpless to stop her precious, fragile core temperature from plummeting.

She'd die betrayed by her own circulatory system. With her heart working to spread ice through her veins, it wouldn't be long before her muscles gave up their pathetic trembling. Not long until the shivering stopped and everything went quiet...

Teeth grit, she clenched her fists, squirming to ease the ache of muscles fast approaching fatigue. Flexing, back arched, she came up against the bonds. Head swimming on an ocean of fizz, ears stuffed with a bizarre, rumbling click.

Drugged. She'd been drugged. That *had*

to be it. The blurry distortion of rational thought tasted like anesthesia, but... aside from the glacier burning through her veins, there were no discernible injuries. No memories of illnesses that would require her to go under the knife.

So why was she here?

Pulling a breath between chapped, cracked lips, she clawed her way back to consciousness. Pressing her shoulder blades into the hard steel beneath her until the bones threatened to slice through her skin and grind themselves dull on the gurney. Relishing the sharp pain and its tethers to the waking world.

A long, low hiss pierced her ears, but *still*, she couldn't pry her lids apart. Could do nothing but tilt her head to the right, trying to pinpoint the sound.

Footsteps, thumping above her head, bringing a second, deeper hiss. A pressure valve letting off steam?

"'Lo?" she slurred, voice ragged and hoarse.

Something wet landed on her sternum. Heavy. Pinning her flat.

She squirmed. "Noo..."

A wordless snarl reverberated through the air, doubling the weight on her chest. Compressing ribs and forcing the air from her lungs. Still beneath the assault, so as not to provoke further retribution, she waited. Counting the seconds.

With a chuff that reverberated the air in her ears, the weight lifted, leaving behind a sticky moisture coating her breasts. Trickling over her sides to pool beneath her armpits. Tingling as it mixed with the chill in the air, it stank of damp, dark things. Neither molding nor rotting, but... musty. As if in need of a good spring clean.

Certainly not something found in the pristine sterility of a modern operating room.

She took a breath, trying to peel her lids apart as feet scuffed the floor by her head.

Picking up a melodic tune, her captor began to hum, voice deep. Masculine. The song unrecognizable, but it was the metallic *clink* that gave her involuntary shivering new life. "Oh, god... Pl-please... let me go..."

The song stopped, mangled by a stream of harsh, guttural words she couldn't comprehend—answered by an airy, light voice hovering by her feet. A voice thick with boredom and contempt, though she couldn't understand the words. But when careless, rough hands found purchase on her inner knees, she knew another sort of *instinctual* language. Primal.

Terror.

Blood rushed in her ears, drowning out the foreign conversation going on above her.

Two. There were two people in the room with her, and the latter stood with what must be a *spectacular* view of her spread nudity. With a squeal, she bucked, trying to pull her knees together by sheer force of will—a useless action driven by panic. She knew that. Understood the mechanics of her organs reacting to the terror signals her brain was sending them. By this point, her adrenal glands had dumped enough hormones into her blood to help her lift a car, or run flat out until she'd beaten every Olympic world record for sprinting and distance ever held.

Useless here, while she was tied to a gurney *not* located in a hospital operating room. Blind and naked. Helpless to resist the man tinkering above her or the woman holding her knees apart as if the cuffs binding her ankles were insufficient. Couldn't fight or flee. No, the adrenaline did nothing but cloud her judgment, when what she truly needed was a plan. A weapon. Some way to get leverage on her captors. Fool them into complacency so they'd give her a chance to *fight*.

Forcing her muscles to still, she exhaled through her nose, focusing on the high-pitched whistle as two streams of air passed over her upper lip. Tickling the tiny, fine hairs on her skin. The tide of rushing blood receded enough that she could pick out the conversation going on around her, punctuated with the clink and *shiiiick* of steel on steel.

Was he sharpening a blade? Preparing to slice into her though he *knew* she was conscious, knew she'd feel it? Was that what he wanted?

Breath in. Breath out. Master the panic—don't let it *be* the master.

"Please," she whispered, licking dry lips, eyeballs rolling behind fused lids. "If you can—can understand me, I have money. I-I'm pretty sure I'm a doctor," she rasped, seizing at the tiny crumb of her broken memory. Not caring whether or not her words were a bluff. "I have a savings account, and—"

Fingers pried her lips apart, plunging past her teeth, palpating the flat of her tongue, then going deeper. Rushing past her gag reflex, in spite of her effort to bite through flesh and bone to stop it.

Slimy.

The wandering digits coated her lips, tongue, and throat in a thick, viscous slime. Probably the same gunk spread across her breasts, though she couldn't see to confirm. She gagged again, abdomen and ribs heaving against the invasion, unable to scream as impossibly long fingers burrowed deeper. Stretching her throat. Making her jaw ache with the force.

Eyes burning, she writhed, trembling beneath him even as his partner moved to pin her hips. But her tears wouldn't fall, trapped as they were behind her eyelids. Which made no sense. Her tear ducts should have been free to function unless her eyes had been *sealed* shut. Glued.

Giving one final, feeble attempt to dislodge his fingers, her diaphragm convulsed, trying to bring oxygen past a blocked airway as carbon dioxide built up in her blood. Behind her lids, shadowed, brilliant stars glittered in the dark. Her brain firing helplessly as oxygen depletion began to settle in.

He withdrew, voice rumbling low and insistent above her as she gasped. Upper back thumping against the gurney with the force of her coughing.

"Unnngh—" She retched, bringing up a mouthful of slime and bile—though she couldn't taste it. Couldn't feel it as it splashed down her chin and chest. Numb. Her tongue was numb. Lips, throat, chest, everywhere the man had touched, everywhere her skin was wet with slime, she was numb. Blessedly so.

Topical numbing agent. Lidocaine, though it didn't taste or smell anything like the product with which she was so dimly familiar. Something similar, perhaps. Something... better. Faster acting. More thorough, for her vocal cords were all but useless now. Paralyzed, barring the smallest, most senseless sounds. Jaw working on wordless air as she tried to force the tiny muscles to work. Tried to scream, to reason with them, to do *anything* but gasp like a fish.

The man laughed, flicking her nose with the tip of a wet finger, cooing and hissing nonsense as he swiped at the mess she'd made of her front. She felt the impact of fingers on her lips without feeling much of anything else. Couldn't stop him when he pried her jaws open once more, tilting her head back and fitting a bit of metal between her teeth. Opening her airway and straightening her throat.

She moaned, trying to shake her head, even as he fitted a clamp around her temples. Pinning her truly immobile and utterly at his mercy. Couldn't move, scream, or thrash.

A shrill, two-toned beep brought a hum from the man and a silky chuckle from his partner. Whatever they were planning, whatever device they were preparing to use on her chirped twice more, then went silent. Leaving a tense, heavy moment in its wake, in which the only sound was her own labored breaths.

When those hated, slender fingers slid down her throat a second time, she could do nothing but take it. Even her gag reflex couldn't be bothered to react to the intrusion, subdued as it was by the slime.

But she could feel him moving inside her. Two long, nimble fingers searching for something. Agitating the delicate cartilage that, if broken, would mean her death.

A click echoed inside her, and for one heart-stopping moment, she assumed it was the sound heralding the end. When that shrill, two-toned beep came from within her, however, she knew.

The device—whatever it was—was inside her.

Grunting, the man shifted his weight, what might have been his belly brushing against her forehead, though whatever caught at her hair was rough. Not skin, then, but something else. A belt, perhaps? Utility pants? Certainly not scrubs she was accustomed to wearing in the operating room, memory intact or not.

The woman murmured something low and soothing, cool, wet fingers tracing the backs of her knees as the beeping started anew. Picking up the pace, chirping a rhythmic tune in place of her voice. Speaking for her.

And then it expanded, making her throat bulge, exceeding the limits of the advanced numbing agent as skin and cartilage shifted, trying to accommodate, lest she tear.

It didn't matter.

With a single, ominous chirp, the thing pierced her throat, popping through the delicate skin above her collarbones. Below her voice box.

Rendered mute, she bucked, eyes bulging behind the lids and rolling in their sockets, she writhed. Sweat beading on every inch of exposed flesh, in spite of the cold. Veins standing out against flushed, warm skin. Pulse pounding in her ears. Unable to scream much less fight for her life.

Another beep. Another spine lancing into the freezing air, slick with blood as it matched the other. Both points of agonizing pain standing out against her collarbones.

Calves flexed, her back bowed. Trying to force the thing out.

Beep.

Pop. Three legs standing rigid in the frost.

A cramp knotted the sole of her left foot, a blissful distraction from the thing playing house in her airway and the sick monsters cooing gentle, loving songs as it moved in.

Beep!

Pop. Skin breaking. Cartilage cracking in an oval around her voice box.

Strong fingers worked at her cramp, kneading the painful, distracting gift away.

Beep!

Five. Five spiny arms waving a gory salute to her captors. And her, without the energy to manage a proper flinch. No, not with the dark stars returning to glimmer at the edge of narrowed vision. Sparkling with the onset of blessed unconsciousness.

Beeeep!

A sixth, and final spine burst through tattered flesh. Her new parasite squawked, shrill, using her throat to speak to its owners.

Humming, the man withdrew his fingers, letting her draw a rattling, ragged breath at last. Preventing her from slipping into the dark as he moved away, he left her trembling on the gurney, pierced and bleeding, airway partially blocked.

He was back before she'd had time to flex

her fingers. Setting something heavy and warm in the center of the spines, speaking in quick, guttural sentences interspersed with whistles and clicks the likes of which she'd never heard before. A rare African dialect, perhaps? Or possibly Amazonian?

The nestling in her throat responded to the man's voice, and with a metallic *click*, the spines snapped shut. Locking in place. One inside, the other out. Some clutching the warm thing they'd been given, while two bent backward to pierce the flesh over her carotid arteries. Seeking better purchase with metal teeth sunk deep, yet they must have avoided a killing blow, for there was no flood of hot life-blood spraying over her nudity. Offering a touch of warmth before her spirit drained away.

No. There was only the pain as the thing burrowed in, getting comfy, clicking and ad-justing its seat over her voice box. Wriggling deep.

Above her, the man spoke. Was answered by the metallic thing poking through her flesh by way of a final, morbid *beeeep!* before it flashed hot. Searing her insides.

But before she could even begin to fight, he tangled those sticky digits in her sweat-damp tresses, and pulled the bit from be-tween her molars. Keeping her motionless as her new voice box sent tendrils of molten steel pulsing throughout her nerves. Into her brain stem and twinning about her spinal cord. Becoming one with her skin, bones, and tendons.

Gentle now, he twisted her head to the left, freeing her from the clamp keeping her immobile and laying her cheek against the gurney and brushed damp hair off her nape.

She groaned, nostrils filled with his musty scent, the copper tang of her own blood, and the charred smoke of pork strip-loin on a hot barbecue. Her own cooked flesh was thick on her tongue, making the empty pit in her stomach beg and whine—which was a degree of morbid she wasn't remotely prepared to cope with.

Not with that faceless man and his female partner mucking around with her vitals. Not when she heard the distinct sound of another metallic *something* being dragged toward her, screeching and scraping on the floor.

It was then, as she lay there staring at the back of her eyelids without the strength to react, that she realized two things. Whatever had been done to her throat was permanent, and she was in shock.

Shock was the only thing capable of explaining why she couldn't be bothered to whimper or fight. Her body's way of protecting her mind when everything else was lost.

All of this should matter. Her heart rate should be elevated to dangerous levels. Palms sweaty. It wouldn't be unexpected if she'd lost control of her faculties at some point, messing all over herself.

But she hadn't. Couldn't bring herself to get too worked up about anything at all.

Perhaps the slime had a sedative effect, even if they'd foregone the courtesy of truly knocking her out during their macabre experiments.

The man was speaking now, soft. His partner responding in kind, though they were both too far away to rouse her. So close… Blissful nothingness only a few seconds away…

He lifted her skull. Bringing her back with a jolt from her inner ear, and she tried to blink through her fused lids when he set something hot against the back of her skull.

It whirred to life, the high-pitched whine of a dentist's drill boring into her skull. Communicating with her new voice box and the searing tendrils branching out beneath her skin. When she heard the click of the two objects joining, she knew it was permanent, even without her sight or being able to speak the language.

But she couldn't bring herself to care. Not when he pressed one of his filthy, sticky fingers to the center of her new voice box and her nerves gave one final, pathetic lurch before they lit up all at once. Sending lightning through her brain as her limbs writhed and danced beneath the kiss of fire at the base of her brain stem.

A strangled, inhuman scream tore itself free from her ravaged throat, numbness be damned. Rupturing something unseen. Gargling blood, she sobbed. Unable to shed her tears. Uncaring if she aspirated and died right then and there, if only someone would take the hot embers out from under her skin!

Panting, she came back to herself. Muscles twitching. Skin warm, in spite of the frigid air.

"They make such pretty sounds, don't they?" A hand traveled down her flank. Caressing. "If this one survives, I think I shall like to have a whole collection of them, dearest."

"Mhm," a man hummed, and a moment later, a warm cloth brushed over her collarbones and throat. "They breed quickly enough. This mammalian species can have litters with as many as—" he paused, as if searching for the information, "—twelve young. Though that's quite rare, according to the directory. Far more likely to have a single pup."

"Yes, well, we can always adjust her birth rate, can't we?" A cluck, and those hands continued petting. Sticky fingers wandering. "Look at all this lovely, stretchy skin! She could carry a *hundred*, if we wanted her to. Just keep her suspended in fluid until the pups are full-term..."

A finger traced her vulva, making her flinch.

"Oh! She's coming around!" the woman cried, elated. "Hurry up. I want to see what color her eyes are. I've heard this species can have a whole *range*."

"She's not *your* pet, Filvtra. You mustn't allow yourself to become attached," he said, but a moment later, applied the cloth to eyes sealed shut, dissolving the solution and returning sight. "Come now, little human. Wakey, wakey."

In spite of the urge to succumb to the day's trauma, his words landed with enough force to keep her conscious. Human. She was *human*. The word rang with truth, giving her a second wind and driving her to do as her tormentor commanded. And with a morbid sort of curiosity, the *little human* did as she was bade.

Then screamed.

ALSO BY MYRA DANVERS

Swallowed by Darkness ~ **FREE**

- Grab your free copy of Swallowed by Darkness now!

The Last Tritan

- Flame to Frost: The Last Tritan, Book I
- Frost to Dust: The Last Tritan, Book II
- Dust to Smoke: The Last Tritan, Book III

Tritan Evolution

- Ravenous Innocence: Tritan Evolution, Book I
- Insatiable Corruption: Tritan Evolution, Book II
- Lavish Destruction: Tritan Evolution, Book III

The Feral Court

- Sinadim: The Feral Court, Book I
- Renegade: The Feral Court, Book II
- Giaus: The Feral Court, Book III
- Sickle: The Feral Court, Book IV

Atom and Evil

- Delirium: Atom and Evil, Book I

MYRA DANVERS

USA Today Bestselling author, Myra Danvers, is best known for her compelling mix of unique science fiction and dark fantasy worlds that feature feisty heroines, antihero men, and of course, proper villains. Though you may not always know who is who until the final pages...

facebook.com/MyraDanvers

instagram.com/myradanvers

bookbub.com/profile/myra-danvers

goodreads.com/httpwwwgoodreadscom-myradanvers

amazon.com/author/myradanvers

tiktok.com/@myradanvers